Marrying Emily

Marrying Emily

Delta Force Heroes

Book 4

By Susan Stoker

Cover Design by Chris Mackey, AURA Design Group
Edited by Kelli Collins & Missy Borucki
Manufactured in the United States

Table of Contents

Chapter One

EMILY SMILED AT her daughter as she nervously and excitedly paced back and forth in the small room. Her white flower girl dress billowed around her with every step, her black combat boots peeking out from under the hem as she walked. She refused to have her hair styled, and the long, dark blonde locks cascaded down her back in artful disarray. The blue bandage on her elbow stood out brightly against the white of her dress, not quite covering all the scrapes she'd gotten that morning after falling on the sidewalk in front of the church. She'd been running around like the wild little girl she was and had tripped.

Luckily, Coach was there to pick her up and find a Skylanders bandage in the church's first-aid kit.

"She's beautiful," Rayne murmured from next to Emily, obviously also watching the little girl.

Emily turned her head to look at her friend. She wasn't sure how close their friendship would be when she'd first met the other woman, but now she couldn't imagine her life without Rayne in it. It was amazing how quickly her circle of friends was growing. She could talk to Rayne concerning her worries about Fletch and his job as a Delta Force operative, and now that Coach had a serious girlfriend, they had another person in their fold as well.

Harley was a video game designer and she'd easily won over Annie with her computer-geek speak. Emily had a feeling Annie would be wanting to follow in the other woman's footsteps when she got older...if she didn't become a soldier.

Mary was also a frequent visitor to their house. She was a bit brash, but it wasn't hard to see it was all a front, and that she was hiding a lot of emotions beneath her gruff exterior. But she loved Rayne unconditionally and would staunchly defend her against any slights. That made Emily love her all the more.

All three women were currently in the room with her. As her bridesmaids, it was their job to keep Fletch away so he didn't see Emily before the ceremony. And he'd tried. Three times.

The first was when they'd arrived at the church. They'd piled out of the limo after getting their hair done at a fancy salon and Annie had spotted Fletch first. She'd screamed his name and had torn off toward him, her arms outstretched.

Mary had grabbed Emily's arm, swung her around

in an Oscar-worthy move and shoved her back into the limo before Emily even knew what was happening.

"What are you doing out here?" Rayne demanded, her body blocking the door to the limo that Emily had just disappeared into. "You know you aren't allowed to see Emily before the ceremony!"

"Hey, ladies," Fletch drawled, holding Annie in his arms on his hip. "I just wanted to make sure you got here all right without any issues."

"We're here and we're good," Mary told him, "so you can just go...wherever...and let us get inside and continue getting ready."

"It was sooooo boring!" Annie declared. "All mommy did was sit there and sit there and sit there while the lady played with her hair."

Fletch chuckled and kissed Annie's temple. "She did, huh? And what about you?"

The little girl shook her head vigorously and repeated, "It was boring."

"She tried," Harley commented. "But even I have to admit...it *was* boring."

Fletch took a step to the side, but Mary copied his movements, blocking his view of Emily...even though there wasn't a chance in hell he'd be able to see anything past the deeply tinted windows on the vehicle.

Rayne reached out for Annie and told Fletch, "Go

on now. We have things to do. You'll see Emily soon enough."

Annie allowed the other woman to take her out of Fletch's arms, but wiggled in Rayne's grasp. She put the little girl down and everyone smiled as she raced off toward the church, yelling Coach's name.

The second time Fletch had tried to sneak in to see Emily, Harley caught him. He was lurking outside the room where they were getting makeup applied, trying to get a glimpse of his fiancée. She slammed the door in his face and made all the women laugh.

The third time, Annie caught him. He'd been inside the women's restroom, waiting for Emily to need to use the facilities so he could sneak a peak...and probably a kiss or two. By then, the little girl had caught on to his game and had screeched in mock-fright and pushed him out of the room. Her little hands on his butt as she scolded him.

Now it was twenty minutes until the ceremony was supposed to start. They were all dressed, made-up, and were simply killing time.

"Was it weird meeting Fletch's parents?" Rayne asked.

Emily immediately shook her head. "No. I thought it would be. I mean, who meets their future in-laws the day before they marry their son? But they were extremely down-to-earth and super friendly.

They apologized for not being able to make it to Annie's adoption ceremony, and were totally sincere about it too."

"Why couldn't they be there?" Harley asked.

Emily turned to the newest member of their girl posse and smiled. Harley's hair was in a dramatic up-do with baby's breath placed here and there. She had a few tendrils framing her face and the navy-blue spaghetti-strap dress looked amazing on her tall, lithe frame.

"His mom was in the hospital. I guess it was some sort of infection that had gotten into her lungs."

"But she's okay now?" Mary demanded.

Emily mentally chastised herself. Mary was extremely sensitive when it came to hospitals and other people being sick. Rayne didn't talk about it much, and Mary *never* brought it up, but they all knew about Mary's bout with breast cancer. Emily wondered if there was something more going on with her, but now definitely wasn't the time to bring it up.

"She's okay now," Emily reassured the other woman. "They wanted to come sooner, but it never really worked out and Fletch didn't want them traveling if his mom wasn't a hundred percent."

"Makes sense," Rayne replied matter-of-factly. "What did they say when they met you though? Seriously, you weren't freaked out?"

"I was," Emily contradicted her earlier statement, "at first. But Annie was there. And since she doesn't really have any grandparents, she was over-the-moon excited to meet them. She broke the ice between us easily."

"Oh man," Mary said softly, not wanting Annie to overhear. "She can get a bit exuberant."

Emily chuckled. "That's the understatement of the year. The second they got out of the car and Fletch said it was okay, she ran toward them, threw her arms around his mom's waist and called her Nana. Then she turned to his dad, did the same thing, and called him Papa. I don't even know where she heard those nicknames. The looks on his parents' faces was priceless."

"He's their only child, right?" Rayne asked.

Emily nodded. "Yeah. I swear to God I saw tears in his mom's eyes. After that, meeting me was a walk in the park."

The women chuckled.

"I can imagine," Rayne said.

"So they spent the afternoon at our house yesterday and slept in the apartment over the garage. They're staying at a hotel tonight. They said they didn't want to impose on our wedding night."

"You seriously aren't going anywhere tonight? I figured you'd for sure go to a hotel in Waco or something," Mary said, her eyebrows raised in question.

Emily shook her head. "No. We decided we wanted the reception to be as low-key as possible. No huge party or anything. And since we're having it at the house, we didn't want to have to drive anywhere afterwards."

"But you *are* going on a honeymoon, right?" Harley asked.

"Oh yeah." Emily smiled huge, thinking about it. "In a couple months, we're going down to Big Bend. It's isolated and there's a lodge that has the cutest little cabins. They don't even have Internet. So we can be totally alone and not have to worry about anything."

"Is Annie going too?" Mary questioned, looking over at the little girl who was playing with a dozen or so small green Army men on the windowsill and muttering to herself.

"She wanted to, but Fletch's parents offered to come back here and stay with her," Emily told her friends.

"And she was okay with that?" Harley asked.

Emily raised her eyebrows and opened her eyes wide, as if to say, "Are you kidding me?"

The women laughed.

"She's okay with that," Harley pronounced, a grin on her face.

"Yeah. She already has them wrapped around her

little finger. Spending four days with her new nana and papa is high on her list of awesome things to happen in her life. So yeah, she's more than okay with it."

"Have you talked about having more kids?" Mary asked in a serious tone that sounded off somehow.

Emily shook her head slowly. "No, not really. I mean, I'm pretty sure Fletch wants more, simply because he's so good with Annie. But I don't think I'm really ready for that yet."

"Take it from me, don't wait. You never know when you'll lose the chance to have kids forever."

The room was silent after Mary's pronouncement. The pain in her tone was clear and the agony on her face was heartbreaking.

"Mary," Rayne began, but before she could continue, there was a loud knock at the door.

"You all about ready in there?" Beatle called out.

Annie left her toys on the windowsill and raced for the door. Before she could throw it open in abandon, Emily quickly called out, "Ask who it is first, baby."

Even though it was obvious who it was, Beatle's southern drawl easily recognizable, Annie paused at the door, her little fingers on the knob, and practically yelled, "Who is it?"

"It's Beatle, sprite," came the reply.

Annie wrenched open the door and screeched,

"Bug man!"

She'd seen him earlier that day, but every time she saw him, she greeted him the same way.

Beatle smiled and held out his arms as Annie leapt into them. He hefted her up and held her tightly as he turned to the ladies. "It's almost time."

His eyes locked on Emily and she could easily see the appreciation in his gaze before he mumbled, "Fletch is a damn lucky man."

Emily blushed. It was silly, but she couldn't help it. Out of all of Fletch's teammates, she knew Beatle and Blade the least, but she knew she was safe with them...with all the guys. As was her little girl. All of Fletch's teammates had babysat Annie at one time or another.

"Thanks," she told him somewhat shyly. "But I think you have it backwards. I'm the lucky woman."

"Whatever," he murmured, then turned his attention back to Annie. "You ready? Where's your basket?"

Annie's head spun around to look for the white, flower girl basket she was supposed to carry down the aisle. If Beatle hadn't been holding on to her tightly, she would've wrenched herself out of his grasp and fallen to the ground. But Beatle, like all the men, was used to her abrupt mannerisms, and kept her from hurting herself.

"It's over there!" Annie said, pointing toward the

window where she'd been playing.

Beatle gently put her back on the ground and told her, "Well, go grab it. It's almost showtime!" Then he looked back up at the women, specifically Emily. "Fletch has been waiting a long time for this day. I'm pleased as I could be for him, Emily."

"Thanks," she said, standing up and walking over to her fiancé's teammate. "Thank you for all you've done for me and Annie. I know it can't be easy to look after her. She's a handful."

Beatle shook his head. "Not at all. She's a delight. I love watching her face light up with excitement when we take her to the base and let her play on the obstacle course. Or when we crawl around in the dirt pretending to be soldiers on a battlefield. She might not be your typical girly-girl, but she has the biggest heart of any child I've ever met. You've done an amazing job in raising her to be exactly who she is, rather than who society wants her to be."

Emily's eyes welled up with tears. It hadn't been easy being a single parent to the precocious little girl. She was too smart for her own good, and it had been an extremely tough road for a while. But with Fletch and all his teammates' attention and love, Annie was growing up to be confident, happy, and outgoing…all while keeping her own sense of self. Emily didn't exactly look forward to when she was a teenager, but she hoped and prayed she'd continue to be the joyful child she was today.

"Thanks, Beatle. That means the world to me."

"You're welcome. Now…shall we go put your fiancé out of his misery? I swear to God he's been grumpy as a pissed-off alley cat. He's not happy he hasn't seen you today. In case you didn't know."

Emily laughed and carefully ran her fingers under both eyes, wiping away the errant moisture, thankful for the waterproof mascara the makeup artist had insisted on. "Yeah, I think I got that."

They both smiled at each other.

"Come on, baby," Emily called to her daughter who was fiddling with her basket by the window.

Annie came running over to her mom and leaned against her side heavily. Emily put a hand on top of her head and smiled down at her lovingly.

Rayne came up on one side of Emily, and Mary on the other. Harley stood next to Mary. Emily looked at her friends. "Let's do this so we can get on to the party."

They all grinned and nodded.

Emily then looked back up at Beatle and gestured to the door with her head. "Lead on, Bug Man. I'm ready to become Mrs. Cormac Fletcher."

Chapter Two

FLETCH FIDGETED IN the tiny room behind the altar. He couldn't pace, there simply wasn't enough room. Not with all of his teammates crammed in there with him. Ghost, Coach, Hollywood, Beatle, Blade, Truck, and the newest member of their clan, Fish, were all watching him with varying degrees of humor, jealously, and delight. The humor because they hadn't seen him this discomfited in a long time, if ever. Jealously, because in a few minutes he'd be tying himself to the woman he loved body and soul, and he wasn't afraid to admit it. Delight for the same reason.

Fish simply looked uncomfortable. It had been Truck's idea to invite the former operative. Dane "Fish" Munroe had belonged to a Delta Force team that had been ambushed over in the Middle East. His arm had been blown off, and Truck and the rest of the team had hauled his ass out of the middle of the destruction and to safety...saving his life in the process.

Fish had been medically retired out of the military

because of his injuries and was currently in rehab. He was pale and held himself stiffly. It was obvious he wasn't sure exactly why he was even there in the first place, but Truck had stubbornly browbeat the man until he'd agreed to attend. And not only that, but to stand up as one of the groomsmen. It wasn't hard to see Fish was adrift. He'd not only lost part of his arm, but his entire close-knit Delta team and his job too.

So Truck had sort of adopted the man. Visiting Fish at the rehab clinic down in Austin every chance he could, talking about his lost teammates, and generally trying to engage him. Having him attend the wedding was just one more way to try to bring him back to the land of the living.

Fletch cocked his head to the side and tugged on the collar of his shirt. The dress blue Army uniform was one he didn't put on often, but he hadn't considered wearing anything else on his wedding day. His friends and teammates were also in theirs, and he had to admit they all looked sharp.

"You ever manage to get a glimpse of Emily today?" Hollywood asked.

"No, dammit," Fletch groused.

"No self-respecting Delta would've failed," Blade teased.

Fletch held his middle finger up to his friend. It wasn't as if he'd *really* tried to see her. Blade was right, if he'd wanted to see his bride before she walked down the aisle, he would've. But he knew the tradition meant a lot to her, and he'd do anything in his power to make this day perfect for the love of his life. So he'd made some halfhearted attempts, which he knew would be rebuffed and hopefully make her laugh. But he could not *wait* to see Emily as she came down the aisle toward him…ready to give herself to him for the rest of her life.

The pastor stuck his head in the door and re-marked, "We're about ready to begin. If you all would follow me and take your places."

Everyone filed out of the room until it was only Ghost and Fletch left. Ghost put his hand on his friend's shoulder and squeezed. "I'm happy for you, Fletch. You and Emily were meant for each other."

"Thanks," Fletch told Ghost. "I know a lot of men dread this moment, or have second thoughts, but I'm so excited to make Emily mine, I feel as if I'm standing in the open door of a plane ready to HALO jump into enemy territory."

Ghost chuckled. "That good, huh?"

"That good. When are you going to make an honest woman out of Rayne?"

Ghost took a step back and looked at Fletch seriously. "I would've married that woman a hundred times by now, but she's not ready."

"What's up?"

Ghost looked toward the door and said quickly, "We don't have time for this right now, but in a nutshell, she's worried about Mary. I don't know what's going on with her best friend, but something is. Maybe a medical setback, with all the doctor's appointments she's going to. But she's too worried about Mary and her possibly having a relapse to even *think* about putting together a wedding."

Fletch put his hand on Ghost's shoulder in support, but didn't say anything.

"But make no mistake, she will be mine. Is, in fact, already mine. I've updated my will, added her to my bank account, and gave her name to the Army as my next-of-kin and she'll get my death benefits. If I had my way, I'd marry her tomorrow, but I respect her and her friendship with Mary enough to wait until she's ready. Rayne is aware I have a ring, she's seen it, so she knows she's it for me. For now, it's enough for both of us."

"It may be old fashioned," Fletch told him, "but there's just something different about knowing your woman is yours legally. Maybe it's cavemanish of me, but there's a part of me that will be relieved when we sign the papers. When I can officially register her with the Army as my wife. Get her ID card, sign her and Annie up for Tricare. I don't know what it is, but it's worth it. As soon as Rayne says she's ready, get it done. You won't regret it."

"I know I won't," Ghost said. "Now, let's go tie you to your woman...yeah?"

"Fuck yeah," Fletch murmured, tugging on the bottom of his uniform jacket. "Let's do this."

FLETCH STOOD AT the front of the church, his eyes wandering the pews as he waited for Emily to appear. He and Emily had decided to keep the guest list small, but the amount of people who'd told him they wouldn't miss his wedding had staggered him.

Of course his teammates, and Fish, were standing up next to him as his groomsmen, but also in the audience were the SEALs who they'd teamed up with in Turkey. Wolf, Abe, Cookie, Mozart, Dude, and Benny were in their dress white uniforms, the stark color standing out amongst the wooden pews and darker colors of the clothing of the other guests.

Penelope "Tiger" Turner, the woman they'd helped rescue from Turkey, was also there. At her side was a man wearing black pants and a blue shirt with a firefighting patch on it. He was tall, almost a foot taller than Tiger, and hadn't taken his hand from the small of her back until they'd been seated. Fletch didn't know who he was, but it was obvious he cared for the woman very much.

Not surprisingly, TJ Rockwell was also there. He was sitting on Tiger's other side. He was in his Highway Patrol uniform. He used to be on a Delta team before chaptering out, and had saved Emily's life from that asshole Jacks. Fletch and his team hadn't worked with him in an official capacity, but once a Delta, always a Delta. He would always be welcome in their fold.

Fletch's eye wandered to another pew to see a man he'd never met until that morning. John Keegan. Tex. *The* Tex. The man was infamous in their top-secret military circles, and had played a part in saving the lives of almost all of the SEALs' women, as well as assisting in situations involving several of TJ's friends.

A pretty woman was sitting next to Tex, her hand resting on his leg. Her blonde hair was pulled back into an elaborate twist at the back of her head and her smile lit up her face. The young baby sleeping in her other arm looked exactly like her. Blonde fuzz on the top of her head, small, delicate. The teenager sitting on her other side couldn't look more different than the couple if she tried. She had dark olive skin, black hair, and was obviously of Middle Eastern decent.

Fletch had learned her name was Akilah, and she was Tex and Melody's adopted Iraqi daughter. He'd only been slightly surprised to note that the teenager had a prosthetic on her arm. Figured Tex, who was missing part of his leg himself, had adopted a teenager with her own missing limb.

At the moment, Akilah's eyes were glued to Fish.

Fletch turned his head and looked at the other Delta out of the corner of his eye. Fish shifted uncomfortably at the end of the row of men standing at the front of the church. His eyes swung from the door at the back, to the windows on either side of the large room. His left arm hung limply at his side, the three-pronged hook of his prosthetic glinting in the bright lights of the church.

Fletch turned his attention back to Akilah and briefly thought that maybe the two would be good for each other in some way.

Before he could dwell further on his friends and family sitting in the audience, the back doors of the church creaked as they slowly opened.

"Wait until you see your little girl and woman, Fletch," Beatle said in a soft voice from his left. "They look amazing."

Without taking his eyes off of the door, straining for that first glimpse of the females he loved more than anything in the world, Fletch whispered, "Shut up, asshole."

He heard all his friends chuckle, but ignored them

as he waited.

Harley was the first to step into the doorway and Coach's indrawn breath was easily heard over the organ music. The woman looked amazing. Like little Annie, she wasn't one to dress up in her everyday life. She was more comfortable in sweatpants and T-shirts than in skirts or dresses, but today she looked amazing.

Her hair was pulled up into some sort of elaborate twist and the white flowers contrasted against the darker color of her curls. The dark blue dress she wore clung to her slender body and shifted as she walked quickly down the aisle. Her steps were fast, as if she hated being the center of attention, which she probably did. Her eyes were glued to Coach's as she walked toward the front of the church, and Fletch saw her mouth, "love you," to Coach before she turned left to take her position at the front of the church.

Emily had been worried that she only had three bridesmaids when he wanted to have seven groomsmen, but in the end they'd decided that they didn't care if they went against tradition and had an uneven bridal party. They'd do their wedding their way, and screw anyone who didn't like it.

Fletch's eyes went back to the door and he watched as Mary started down the aisle next. Her hair was cut short, and thus couldn't be styled exactly, but she had a clip in her hair that had rhinestones on it, which sparkled as she walked toward them.

Curious as to his friend's reaction, Fletch turned his head and saw Truck gazing at Mary with a look that had both longing and concern written all over it. The longing, Fletch understood; it was more than obvious that the biggest, meanest, roughest man on their team was smitten with the diminutive, prickly best friend of Rayne's, but the concern was a bit harder to place. Anyone who was around Mary for five minutes could see that the woman could take care of herself, and *wanted* to.

Even though there had been some secretive phone calls back and forth between Truck and Mary, Fletch didn't know where the concern was coming from. He didn't have time to wonder any more about it though, as Mary took her place next to Harley.

Then it was Rayne's turn to walk down the aisle. Her job as a flight attendant meant that she was more outgoing than the other women in their group. And impressively, the hell she went through in Egypt had somehow made her more mentally tough rather than breaking her. Rayne smiled at Ghost as she came toward him, the love for him clear in her eyes.

Fletch couldn't hold back the wide smile on his face as he turned his eyes to the back of the church. The time he'd been waiting for was here. Annie.

He'd seen his daughter earlier, when he'd let her

"catch" him in the restroom waiting for Emily. She looked adorable and he wouldn't change one thing about her outfit. The white dress she was wearing was frilly, lacy, and poofed out from her waist, falling to the floor in what seemed like miles of material. It was so incongruent to what the little girl normally wore, he wouldn't have bet she'd wear it in a million years.

His daughter hated girly things. Loathed them. But because her mom was going to be wearing white, and because her daddy asked her to, Annie had agreed to wear the dress. But only to the wedding itself. Not the reception. Both he and Emily had immediately agreed, not caring what she wore afterwards. But then they'd gone further, deciding that it was a great idea, and no one was allowed to wear their "fancy duds" to the party. No uniforms, no cocktail dresses. Everyone had been instructed to change into comfortable clothes before they showed up at their house for the reception.

But it was the small combat boots on Annie's feet that Fletch loved the most. They were so Annie. Truck had bought the boots, had them specially made for her adoption ceremony. She'd worn them almost every day since. One night, while she'd watched Fletch polishing his dress shoes for the wedding ceremony, she'd insisted on Fletch showing *her* how to polish her own boots. So he'd taught his daughter how to buff, polish, and shine her boots, while he did the same with his shoes. It wasn't exactly the father-daughter activity he thought he'd be engaging in, but he'd take it.

Annie smiled at him from the end of the aisle and she started toward him slowly, as she'd been trained. Her tongue stuck out in concentration as she picked a flower petal from her basket and dropped it on the floor. Her eyes were glued to her basket, trying not to mess up.

Fletch smiled. Her hair was wild around her face and shoulders, hanging loose. It was interesting that for a girl who eschewed anything feminine, she wouldn't let anyone cut her long hair. He was thankful for that, because she had beautiful hair. Long, shiny, and thick. Yes, it was messy at the moment, but it was totally Annie.

Fletch heard the chuckles start from the back of the church and slowly move forward as Annie continued down the aisle. He wasn't sure what everyone was laughing at until Ghost leaned into him and whispered, "Look at what she's dropping in the aisle."

Fletch's eyes went from his daughter to the floor behind her—and he almost choked, trying to keep his chuckle from erupting.

Annie was dropping white flower petals, as she'd been instructed, but she was also dropping little green Army men. She'd reach into her basket, pull out a petal and drop it, then reach in and pull out an Army man. She continued down the aisle, alternating between sprinkling the floor with flowers and the toys.

As much as he wanted to scold her for being mischievous, he couldn't. It was so freaking adorable. He worried about Emily stepping on one of the plastic toys and twisting an ankle though.

As soon as the thought went through his head, Dude, one of the SEALs, moved.

He was already sitting toward the back of the room, but he quickly walked back up the aisle and unobtrusively brushed the toys to the side of the aisle as he went, standing at the back of the church when he got to the end so as not to bring any more attention to himself.

Fletch relaxed. He didn't know the SEAL team that well, but it was obvious Dude was the kind of man who took extreme care of his woman. Fletch would bet everything he owned the man had a daughter...one he was extremely protective of.

Annie got to the end of the aisle and beamed up at Fletch. "Hi, Daddy Fletch!" she said loudly. "I'm sooooo ready for you and mommy to get married. I mean, you're already sleeping in the same bed, so that won't change, but now mommy will be 'Fletch' too."

Fletch felt the sheen of a blush make its way from the back of his neck through his cheeks and tried to ignore the chuckles from the men standing on his left.

He went down on one knee and held out his arms to his daughter. Annie dropped her basket, flower petals and the few Army men that were left inside spilling out onto the altar, and threw herself into Fletch's arms.

Fletch wrapped his arms around her small body and held her to him, inhaling the little girl smell of her as he buried his face into her neck. "I love you, sprite."

"I love you too, Daddy."

"Now, go stand next to Rayne and let's get this done, yeah?"

"Yeah," Annie said, nodding enthusiastically. "Let's get this done!" She ran back to her basket and kneeled down, her dress billowing out around her as she shoved the Army men back into the basket, ignoring the flower petals in a lump on the floor, then ran toward Rayne, shoving in between her and Mary.

The music changed to the "Wedding March," all the guests stood and turned, and Fletch's eyes whipped from the antics of his daughter to the entrance at the end of the aisle. The doors had been shut and two people—Fletch had no idea who they were, not that he cared—were standing there, each with a hand on a handle, ready to open them and admit Emily.

As if in slow motion, Fletch watched as the men stood back, opening the doors. The entryway was empty for a moment, before Emily stepped from the side into the doorway in all her wedding splendor.

Fletch's breath hitched and he knew he actually gasped as he laid eyes on his bride for the first time. He hadn't seen her dress before now, and it was absolutely stunning.

The front had a deep vee, showing off a hint of cleavage. The lace hugged her waist, outlining every curve of her delightful body. The lace extended from the bodice down her arms, covering her, but showing off her tanned skin beneath. The skirt flared out from her waist and hips into a slight train behind her. The flowers clutched in her grip were calla lilies, a simple and elegant bouquet. Fletch couldn't see the back of her head and hairdo, but he knew it was complicated because she'd been at the beauty parlor for two hours earlier that day getting it done.

But it was the smile on her face and the anticipation and love in her gaze that drew him in the most. She kept her eyes on him as she slowly walked down the aisle. They'd talked about if she wanted to have his dad walk her down the aisle, as her own parents were deceased, but she'd declined, saying she was perfectly able to walk down the aisle by herself...besides, no one was giving her away, she was giving *herself* to him.

Fletch couldn't take his eyes off her as she came toward him, just as hers stayed glued to his. About halfway down the aisle, she stumbled, surprise and horror showing in her face as she caught herself and stayed upright. Fletch's feet were moving before he'd even thought about it. He vaguely noticed that three of the SEALs—plus TJ, the firefighter at Tiger's side, and a few other men—had also shifted, as if they too were about to come to her aid.

But he got to Emily before anyone else, sliding his arm around her slender waist and pulling her into his side. He leaned down and said in her ear, "Our daughter decided to adorn the aisle with her precious Army men as well as flowers."

Emily's eyes sparkled as she looked up at him. "I'd expect nothing less."

The music continued in the background, but Fletch only had eyes for the woman he loved with all his heart. "You look beautiful."

"So do you," she returned immediately, softly.

Fletch didn't know how long they would've stood there, staring at each other, but luckily Wolf, the leader of the SEALs, leaned into the aisle and said loudly, "We don't have all day, man. You can eyeball her later. You've got vows to say!"

Fletch lifted his chin to the man, then turned back to Emily. He took a step back, held out his elbow and bowed slightly. "If I might escort you to the altar, my love?"

Emily immediately wrapped her hand around his arm and pressed into his side as she looked up at him and responded, "Please."

So they walked arm in arm down the rest of the aisle until they reached the pastor, who was smiling widely at them, not looking at all put out at the delay or change in procedure. Fletch smiled over at Annie and winked, delighted when she awkwardly winked back at him.

Rayne took the bouquet from Emily and the pastor didn't waste any time getting on with the ceremony. If asked, Fletch couldn't have said what the man talked about, but figured it was the usual wedding ceremonial talk. All he could see was the love in Emily's eyes when she gazed at him. All he could feel was the warmth of her body in front of his as he held her hands tightly in his own. All he could hear was his own quick breathing as he anxiously waited for his turn to say his vows.

Then finally it was time.

The pastor turned to him and said, "I understand you have written your own vows to each other."

He and Emily nodded at the same time.

The pastor nodded in return, then put his hands behind his back and waited for Fletch to begin.

Emily had brought up the subject of them reciting their own vows to each other, and at first Fletch wasn't that excited about the idea. He wasn't sure what he should say and didn't think he could match anything

Emily came up with. But at the look of disappointment on his fiancée's face, a look she'd tried to hide, he'd capitulated.

And now he was glad. He couldn't wait to tell Emily, all his friends and family, and God, exactly how much and what this moment meant to him.

He turned to Emily and took both her hands in his. He bought them up to his mouth and gently kissed the back of each one, resting his lips on the second one for a long moment before he looked into her eyes and spoke.

"Emily, you know I'm a practical man. A soldier. It's all I've ever been and all I thought I would ever be. But from the moment you knocked on my door, asking if the apartment was still available, I've been a changed man. It's as if the romantic and sappy side of me was just waiting for you to come into my life. Every minute of every day, I think about you. Where you are. What you're doing. *How* you're doing. Are you smiling, laughing, crying... I hate every second I miss of your beautiful smile and I absolutely loathe the times when I'm working and can't be with you because I know you're worrying about me. But one thing you never have to worry about, is whether or not I love you. Every day I wake up with you by my side, I have to pinch myself to make sure you're not a figment of my imagination. Every time I see you laughing and smiling with our daughter, I'm reminded of how lucky I am. There will be hard times, times we argue, times we're upset with each other, and even times when we're sick or hurting, but know to the bottom of your heart, that *my* heart belongs to you though it all.

"I will never stray from you. Ever. You're the only woman I want, now and forever. I will never break your trust in me. Never gossip about you. Never blame you for anything that might happen in the future. And if I'm taken away from you,"—Fletch ignored the tears that had been in her eyes for the last few moments, but at his words, tumbled over and ran down her flushed cheeks—"know that I did everything in my power to fight to stay. To get back to you and Annie. Not only that, you might be marrying me today, but you're getting seven other protectors,"—he motioned behind him to his Delta teammates and Fish, but never lost eye contact with Emily,—"who will move heaven and earth to give you and our daughter, and any future children we might have, whatever you need. You're not only marrying me today; you're marrying into a large family. Getting a mom and dad, seven brothers, and Annie is getting seven uncles. I love you, Miracle Emily Grant. More than I ever thought possible."

Fletch had more to say, but he was done. His voice had cracked on the last line of his vow to her, and the tears coursing down his love's face had done him in.

Emily clutched at his hands then fell into his chest. Her face buried into his dress uniform and she sniffed loudly. Fletch dropped her hands and wrapped his arms around her, one hand resting on the small of her back and the other on the buttons of her dress that ran down her spine. Her own hands clutched his back as they wound around him.

The pastor, and all their friends watching, gave them time and space to work through the emotions they were both feeling. Finally, the pastor cleared his throat, and Emily pulled back. Rayne stepped forward and handed her a handkerchief and Emily dabbed at her eyes and cheeks, trying not to ruin her makeup.

She handed the handkerchief back to her maid of honor, glanced at the pastor, who nodded, and she took a deep breath, before clutching Fletch's hands as she'd been before they'd been overcome with emotion.

"I *so* should've gone first," she muttered with a small grin. A few chuckles sounded from those nearest them who had overheard. Then she said louder, "I love you. I'd been alone so long that I'd forgotten what it felt like to trust. To lean on someone else. You gave that back to me...and then some. I figured I'd wait until Annie had grown up before maybe trying to date again, but the second I saw you, I trusted you. Even though we had a massive communication breakdown, I trusted you. I didn't move out, because I somehow knew you wouldn't hurt us. When we were taken, I trusted you to find us. When you said you wanted to adopt Annie, I trusted you, even though we weren't married yet. When you leave to go to work, I *do* trust that you'll do everything in your power to come home to me and our daughter. I trust your friends to have your back just as you'll have theirs. All my life, I've never trusted anyone but myself. Cormac Fletcher, I'll be true to you every single day we have together. I will love you through thick and thin. Through sickness and health."

Her eyes moved then, gazing past him to Dane Munroe, standing stock still at the end of the line of groomsmen, and she said, "If you come home missing a limb, or wounded, I'll love you no less."

Her eyes came back to his.

"In fact, I'll love you *more*, because I'll know how hard you fought to come home to me. I love you, and this is the happiest day of my life."

At the conclusion of her vows, Emily turned and held out her hand to Annie, who quickly stepped forward.

Fletch's eyebrows rose. This wasn't part of their rehearsed plan.

"And it's the bestest day of my life too," Annie chimed in, snuggling in next to her mom and gazing up at Fletch. "Well, except for the day you officially became my daddy, but this is a pretty darn close second."

Everyone laughed, but Annie ignored them and continued. "My mommy is the best. She couldn't be a better mommy. But since the day we met you and moved into your garage apartment, she's been even better. Thank you for loving us. Thank you for wanting to be my daddy. And thank you for making an honest woman out of my mommy."

Fletch couldn't hold back his grin. Annie heard and retained the strangest things...usually spouting them off at the most inopportune times. Like now. He ignored the choked laughter of the pastor and kneeled down to take Annie's hands in his own.

"I vowed to always love and respect your mother, sprite, and I do the same to you. I'm not only marrying your mom today, but I'm tying the three of us together officially. You were already my daughter, Annie Elizabeth Grant Fletcher, but today just makes it doubly official."

"Cool," Annie breathed.

"Yeah, cool," Fletch echoed. Then he reached for her and hugged her tightly before letting go and standing up.

Annie smiled up at both of them, and said in a loud whisper to her mom, "Now's the good part, Mommy...you get to kiss him!" Then she stepped back into her place next to Rayne as the congregation once again tried to hold back their laughter.

Fletch, his eyes shining with mirth, stepped closer to Emily, but looked to the pastor in expectation.

"I guess that's my cue. Cormac Fletcher. Miracle Emily Grant. By the power invested in me by the state of Texas, I now pronounce you man and wife. You may kiss your bride," he told Fletch.

Without delay, and ignoring the clapping and cat calls from his friends, Fletch took Emily's head between his hands, loving how her chin came up to make it easier for him and her own hands encircled his wrists, further binding them together, and he leaned down.

Whispering, "I love you," Fletch covered his wife's lips with his own. Everyone else ceased to exist for him as he kissed his wife for the first time. Emily immediately opened under him, letting him take her mouth the way he wanted. Deep, hard, and wet.

When he finally pulled back, her eyes were shining, her face was flushed, and he could tell she was just as aroused as he was. Emily licked her lips and squeezed his wrists affectionately.

"Mr. and Mrs. Cormac Fletcher!" the pastor boomed.

Fletch took the cue—even though he wanted nothing more than to sate the lust he saw in his wife's eyes, and that he knew was shining in his own—and turned them to face the audience. Rayne shoved the bouquet in Emily's arms and Annie leaped around them to Fletch's other side. He grabbed on to his daughter's hand, kept his arm around his wife's waist, and all three of them walked back down the aisle together as an official family at last.

Chapter Three

"FLETCH, STOP. WE can't. Everyone is waiting for us," Emily halfheartedly complained to her new husband.

She'd had some good kisses from her husband. Some great ones. But the one he'd given her right after they'd been declared man and wife would be one she'd never forget as long as she lived. It had been hot, and she physically felt the love pour into her as his tongue had dueled with her own. If they hadn't been standing in front of God and everyone, she would've begged him to take her right then and there.

But they *had* been and afterward they'd had to greet the guests as they'd left the church, then take pictures. But now they were finally alone. Rayne and Ghost had taken Annie back to the house, promising to help her get changed into jeans and T-shirt. Everyone else was meeting them back at their house.

The caterers were supposed to have everything already set up. The newly married couple needed to give everyone time to get back to the house so they could make their grand entrance.

They'd stashed the clothes they were going to change into for the reception at Mary's apartment. They were going to change back at the house, but Mary told them in no uncertain terms that they couldn't be there when the guests arrived. It just wasn't done. Tradition stated they had to be announced as they entered the reception as Cormac and Emily Fletcher. Mary had insisted on them changing at her apartment, *then* making their way back to their house and the reception.

But apparently Fletch had something else on his mind than worrying about if his friends were waiting on them. The second they'd let themselves into the apartment, Fletch's hands were all over Emily.

"I can't stop," he said between kisses. "You have no idea how much I want to be inside you."

Emily flushed with excitement. Even though they'd made love the night before, she'd never get enough of Fletch. She shivered as his lips trailed over the nape of her neck even as his fingers were nimbly undoing the delicate buttons at her back. One by one he loosened each of them, while nipping and licking at the sensitive skin of her neck.

Emily moaned and reached around to grip his hips as her gown slowly gaped open.

Fletch's chin rested on her shoulder as one arm

snaked around her waist and pulled her back against his chest. "Are you wearing a corset?" he asked huskily, his eyes glued to her breasts, which were in full view now that her dress had been undone.

"Uh huh," she affirmed distractedly.

"Fuck me," he swore softly.

"I would if you'd hurry up," Emily responded cheekily, spinning in his arms until she faced him.

Without a word, Fletch put both hands on her shoulders and slowly pushed the beautiful white lace dress down her arms. It fell to the floor in a whoosh of material, pooling around their feet unnoticed.

Fletch's eyes went from Emily's breasts, plumped up by the corset, down to her waist, to the white panties and garter belt holding up the white stockings on her legs. Then they moved back up, but stopped once more at her boobs.

Emily chuckled. Fletch was awesome at not making her feel like he only wanted to be with her for sex, but at the moment she was beyond thrilled that he wasn't able to tear his eyes away from her body. It made her feel sexy and even more horny.

She reached for the buttons on his dress blue uniform. "Take this off, honey," she urged.

Without taking his eyes from her chest which was rapidly moving up and down with her quickening breaths, he absently undid the buttons on his jacket, the tie around his neck, the cufflinks at his wrists, and the first few buttons of his crisp white shirt.

While he was busy disrobing, Emily went to work on his pants, unbuckling his belt and unzipping the zipper. She took a step into him, shoved her hands under the material of his pants, cupped his butt briefly, and pushed. His pants cascaded to his feet just as her dress had.

As if he'd been waiting for exactly that, Fletch moved. He tugged her into him so they were hip to hip and devoured her mouth. They twisted their heads back and forth, trying to get deeper inside one another.

Fletch picked her up until her feet were dangling off the floor, and not breaking their kiss, he kicked off his shoes and pants, then took three steps until her back was against the wall.

He lifted his head from hers only long enough to say, "Wrap your legs around me, Em."

She immediately did as he'd ordered, clutching his hips with her thighs. She wanted him inside her more than she wanted her next breath. She could feel the wetness against her panties.

Fletch hitched her higher and leaned down until he could reach her chest. He brought one hand up and tugged a cup of the corset until her breasts popped out the top. Emily looked down and thought she seemed a bit obscene…her nipples hard and her white, creamy boobs pushed up by the lingerie, but before she could feel embarrassed or shy, Fletch covered one with his mouth and the other with his hand.

Throwing her head back until it thunked against the wall, Emily inhaled. She grabbed the back of Fletch's head and pushed him into her, encouraging him to suck on her nipple harder. He acquiesced immediately and Emily felt another trickle of wetness seep out of her core. She pressed against his erection and moaned. "Please, Fletch."

He lifted his head and asked, "Please what?"

"Fuck me," Emily said immediately. "I need you inside me so bad."

Without a word, Fletch braced her upper back on the wall and ordered, "Hold on to me."

She did, wrapping both arms around his shoulders and clutching the back of his neck.

Fletch's eyes met hers for the first time since he'd removed her dress. The heat and love in them made her squeeze her legs around him reflexively. She felt his hand between them, pushing his boxers down to free his cock.

Then she felt the gusset of her panties being pushed to the side and one long finger press inside her. She gasped at his thick finger pushing its way into her body, but didn't close her eyes. Fletch added another finger, and Emily knew he was making sure she could take him without pain. The last thing he ever wanted to do was hurt her. The tattoos on his arm rippled sexily as his hand moved inside her.

"You're so wet," he observed unnecessarily.

"Because I want my husband to fuck me," Emily said, huskily and impatiently.

His fingers disappeared and she felt the tip of his cock press against her core. As Fletch pushed inside her and they made love for the first time as husband and wife, he said, "My wife," with such reverence it made tears well in her eyes.

She could only nod as no words would squeeze past the lump in her throat.

He took her then. Slow and easy at first, then harder and faster. They hadn't taken the time to get fully undressed, she was still wearing the two-inch heels on her feet, and the elastic of her underwear dug into her skin with every thrust of her husband's cock inside her, but Emily didn't feel any of it. All she felt was the intense love coming from Fletch as they gazed into each other's eyes as they made love.

As usual, Emily broke first, closing her eyes and throwing her head back as she orgasmed. Her muscles strangling Fletch's dick as he strained to push in and out of her body. She opened her eyes just in time to see his orgasm come over him. Every muscle got tight, his eyes squeezed shut, and his hands clutched her ass so tightly Emily knew she'd probably have finger-sized bruises on it for the next few days. He held her hips against him as he shuddered and shook, then emptied himself inside her.

When he was done, his eyes opened and he grinned down at her. "Fuck, I needed that."

Emily giggled and leaned forward and kissed him on the lips, fast and hard. "Me too. But now we *really* need to get going. Everyone is waiting for us to get back to the house."

"Are you gonna tell Mary we fucked for the first time as man and wife in the hallway of her apartment?"

Emily's eyes widened in horror. "No!"

Fletch chuckled and shrugged. "No matter. I think she's gonna know anyway."

Emily smacked his upper arm, knowing there was no way she could hurt him. "Shut up. Let me down so I can change."

Reluctantly, Fletch pulled out of her body and let her slide down the wall until her feet touched the ground. He put his hand over her pussy and massaged her for a moment. "Leave all of this on."

"All of what?" Emily asked, distracted because of the sweet way he was holding her. He wasn't trying to turn her on, wasn't pressing his fingers into her. He was just cupping her bare flesh inside her panties.

"The corset. The panties, the hose. All of it. It's fucking sexy and I want to take my time tonight, removing it piece by piece and making sure my wife knows how much her effort was appreciated."

Emily laughed and said, "I think she knows," then gasped as she felt some of his come slide out of her body.

Fletch's hand moved then, massaging their combined essence into her skin. It should've been gross, but she'd gotten used to how much Fletch loved to feel the evidence of their lovemaking. She'd complained once about how the aftereffects of having sex sucked for the woman, and he'd countered by saying, "I'd love to be able to feel you on me hours after we made love. I'm jealous you have that and I don't."

So now, more often than not after he'd pull out, he'd massage her so he could share in the feeling of his seed leaking out of her body. When they were in bed, she'd stopped cleaning up right after they made love, falling asleep with his hand cupping her tenderly.

Reluctantly, he removed his hand and said, "Go clean up. I know you don't want to feel sticky throughout the reception."

Looking around as she pulled away and headed for the bathroom, grabbing the bag of clothes she'd placed in the hallway that morning before heading to the salon, Emily shook her head at the mess around them. Her dress lay abandoned, his shoes, pants, and uniform were strewn about the small entryway. She chuckled. Mary wouldn't care they'd had sex in her apartment. She probably expected it.

As she cleaned up and got dressed, Emily giggled, suddenly realizing that Fletch had made love to her still wearing his boxers *and* socks. There were worse things in life than having a man so in love with you he couldn't even wait to get all the way undressed before he had to take you.

AN HOUR LATER, Emily was laughing with Rayne and Harley as she drank a mixed drink. She had no idea what it was, but the bartender they'd hired for the reception had been given strict orders to make sweet alcoholic drinks for the ladies, and to keep the beer flowing for the men. And so far, he'd been doing an excellent job, even going so far as to make Annie and Akilah virgin versions of the cocktails the adults were drinking.

Emily's eyes wandered the backyard, smiling at each group of people she saw. The day had been great, but the evening had been perfect. Seeing all the men and women who were involved in both her and her husband's lives was amazing.

Fletch had hired a lawn company to overhaul the yard and make it both presentable and comfortable. They'd mowed the grass, added a firepit with a few benches, and an awning to the porch. It looked professional and neat…it was a perfect setting for their reception as well as the many barbeques they liked to throw.

Most people were wearing jeans or cargo pants and either T-shirts or polos. Emily was wearing a black pair of slacks and a long-sleeve purple shirt. It was silky and every time Fletch put his hands on her, the material slid along her skin sensually.

It was a laid-back setting and everyone was smiling and laughing. Emily looked over to where Fletch was sitting and caught him grinning back at her. She lifted her chin at him, and ran her fingers up and down the collar of her shirt, teasing him. His eyes narrowed at her actions and she laughed.

"Would you quit teasing the poor man," Rayne said, exasperated.

"But it's so much fun," Emily responded, tearing her eyes away from Fletch with difficulty.

"Who are the men he's talking to again?" Harley asked.

"Those are the SEALs," a feminine voice cut in from their right. It was Penelope, the firefighter from

San Antonio. "They were the men who rescued me from Turkey."

"Ah." Harley nodded.

"I'm Penelope," she told Emily and Harley. "We haven't met yet."

The three women all shook hands.

"It's really good to officially meet you," Emily told her. "I've heard a lot about you from Fletch and the other guys."

Penelope wrinkled her nose, then smiled.

"All good, promise," Emily reassured her.

"The SEALs also paired up with our Delta guys when that shit went down in Egypt," Rayne chimed in after the introductions were done. "I vaguely remember them from when I was rescued, but honestly, it's all pretty much a blur. How are you doing?" Rayne asked Penelope gently. They'd gotten together and talked, having being kidnapped in common.

The smaller woman shrugged. "Some days are better than others."

"Who's the hottie fireman who's barely left your side since we got here?" Emily asked her with a smile.

Penelope looked around unconsciously, finding Tucker "Moose" Jacobs across the lawn. He was talking with TJ and looking extremely relaxed. Though he still had on the black slacks he'd been wearing at the ceremony, he now had on a navy-blue

T-shirt with a small Station 7 Firestation logo on the left breast. "It's not like that," Penelope protested somewhat weakly.

"Riiiiiiight," Rayne drawled. "Just as it's not like that between Mary and Truck...right?" She gestured to the couple sitting off to the side, having what looked like an intense conversation.

Penelope shrugged, but she had a small smile on her face. "Moose thinks I'm weak and need my hand held all the time. Even though I was a soldier and have been a firefighter forever."

"I don't believe he thinks you're weak," Harley noted seriously. "I don't know you, but from an outsider's view, it looks to me more like he's standing by your side just *in case* you need him. He comes across as watchful as opposed to anything else and lets you do your own thing more often than not. And if *I* can tell you're struggling with demons, he can too."

No one said anything for a moment, and finally Penelope demurred, "I'm not weak, but I have to admit there are times when my demons overwhelm me. A couple of times it's happened when he's been around." She looked down and played with the condensation on her glass. "He was...helpful."

The women nodded, knowing exactly what Penelope was talking about. They'd all been there. "Thank you for coming up," Emily told the other woman, putting a hand on her arm. "I've heard about you from Rayne so it's great to finally meet you in person."

"Your husband is a wonderful man," Penelope told her. "I'll never be able to thank any of them enough."

"None of them expect thanks," Rayne said matter-of-factly.

"I know, but I like to say it nevertheless."

All the women nodded in agreement. They'd never be able to repay the Deltas. Ever.

TRUCK LEANED INTO Mary and asked, "What did the doctor say?"

Mary shrugged and refused to meet Truck's eyes. "Nothing new."

"What does that mean?" Truck insisted, putting his large hand on her knee.

She finally looked at him and did her best not to cry. This was Emily's wedding. A happy occasion. Not time for her to burst out in tears. "They're still doing tests, but he's pretty sure the cancer has returned."

"You need to tell Rayne," Truck said gently.

Mary shook her head vigorously. "I can't. I can't do that to her."

"Why not? She's your best friend. She'd do anything for you."

"I know she would, but I don't *want* her to. I think my having cancer hurt *her* more than it did me. She was so devastated and stuck by me every step of the way. She took time off from work that she couldn't afford to lose because she refused to let me go to any of my appointments by myself. I leaned on her way too much, and I don't want to be that kind of friend ever again. The type who takes more than she gives."

"You give more than anyone I've ever known," Truck told her gently.

Mary shook her head sadly. "No I don't. Look how mean I always am to you."

"I can take what you dish out, Mary," Truck said. "I actually find it refreshing that you aren't scared of my looks or size like most people are."

Mary looked across the lawn to where Rayne was standing talking to Emily, Harley, and Penelope. "I'm not scared of you, Truck. There are worse things to be afraid of in this world, but I shouldn't be such a bitch."

Truck took her chin in his hand and turned her face to his. "Can I be honest?"

Mary eyed the large man in front of her. Her skin tingled where his fingers touched her. Every time he did she felt electrified. She wanted this man more than she'd ever wanted anything in her entire life. But she couldn't have him. She had no idea if she'd be alive in the next year, so there was no way she could start anything with him. It wouldn't be fair. "Please. I'd prefer you always be honest with me."

"It turns me on."

"What?"

"You being bitchy. Calling me 'Trucker' while you sneer at me...it turns me on."

Mary narrowed her eyes at him. "There's no way. That's insane."

Truck let go of her face and sat back, taking a sip of his beer before saying, "Look at me, Mary." He gestured to his face.

"I'm looking."

"I'm hideous."

Mary's stomach rolled but she shook her head and her lips tightened in irritation. "You are not," she barked at him.

"I have a mirror, Little Bit. I know what I look like. My scar is awful." He ran his finger across the red, jagged skin on his cheek. The blemish ran from under his eye, down his cheek, to the corner of his lips. It pulled his mouth down so it looked like he was perpetually scowling. "You're the only female since it happened to not give a shit about my scar. Well, you and Annie. The first time she met me, she put her little hand on my face and asked me if it hurt. I'd do anything for that little girl. Anyway, you got right up in my face and gave me shit. My cock got so hard I thought for sure you'd take one look and be horrified. But you didn't even notice. You just *kept* giving me shit and coming at me because you were worried about Rayne. It was awesome."

Mary just stared at Truck. If she was honest with herself, his scar *was* horrible. It was puckered and painful looking. But after her initial shock of imagining the violence that caused the blemish on his face, she'd stopped noticing it. She'd seen enough breast cancer survivors, burn victims, and other disfigured people during her time in various hospitals that the mark on his face no longer really even registered. And over the last few months, he'd been the person she'd turned to more and more. Rayne was her best friend, and *would* always be, but Rayne had Ghost now. Mary couldn't, and wouldn't, drag her down into her life of medical appointments and cancer scares again.

She didn't want to drag *anyone* down, but Truck didn't seem to care. He did what he wanted no matter what she said. It had annoyed her at first, but lately she'd come to expect him to simply ignore her when she said she didn't need his help. Slowly but surely, she'd started to rely on him just as much as she'd once relied on Rayne.

"I'm more concerned with who you are inside than what you look like on the outside." Mary told him. "I don't see your scar when I look at you."

"I know you don't. And it means the world to me. When's your next appointment?"

Mary blinked at the abrupt change in subject. She thought he'd ask her what she saw in him. Figured he'd say something to keep her on her toes. "Next week," she told him. "But I'm not sure I'm going."

"What do you mean? You have to go," Truck said, appalled.

Mary sighed. "My insurance won't pay for any more cancer treatments. My company changed our benefits and they're saying the treatment's not covered, or something like that. I don't really understand it all. But it doesn't really matter. I'm tired, Truck. Tired of fighting."

"Don't you fucking give up." Truck scowled at her.

"I can't afford it," she told him honestly. "It exhausts me even thinking about how the hell I'll pay for chemo and radiation without insurance."

"I'll figure something out," he told her immediately.

"Truck, this isn't something you—"

"You are *not* giving up. You *will* get the treatment you need and you will beat this again. Got it?" Truck told her fiercely. He wasn't touching her, but he was leaning into her, getting into her personal space.

"Okay," she agreed. How could she do anything else with him in her face like he was?

"I'm going with you to your next appointment," Truck said, sitting back and giving her a little bit of breathing room.

Mary shook her head automatically. "No."

"Yes," Truck countered. "No matter how this turns out, I'll be by your side."

"Truck, you can't—"

"I can," he interrupted. "And I will."

Mary glared at him. If she let him do this, help her through this like Rayne did the last time she'd been sick, he'd get under her skin even more than he already was. She refused to let that happen. The last thing she wanted was to fall in love with the man. If she somehow gained the only thing she'd always wanted, to be loved, only to know she wouldn't get to fully experience it because she was dead, would suck.

So she did what she'd always done—she turned on her inner bitch…simply to get Truck to decide she wasn't worth the trouble. She had to protect her heart no matter what. "I said no, *Trucker*. I don't need you to hold my hand like I'm a fucking baby." She slammed her drink down on the table next to her. "As if I'd want a big freak like you by my side. You'd scare everyone away."

Instead of getting pissed as she'd intended, Truck

merely smiled. "Good. Because you're mine. If anyone even *thinks* about giving you shit, they'll have to deal with me."

Scared about how good his words made her feel, and how much he made her crave having him by her side to lean on if she had to go through another cancer scare, Mary forced herself to roll her eyes and storm away. Fuck, she was in big trouble.

ON THE OTHER side of the party, Akilah held her baby sister, Hope, in her arms while their parents swayed back and forth on the makeshift dance floor in the middle of the lawn.

Tex and Melody had adopted her when she had nowhere else to go, and some days she couldn't believe how different and wonderful her life was now than when she'd lived in war-torn Iraq.

She still missed her parents, they'd been killed by an explosive planted by the Taliban in her village, the same explosive that had taken her arm, but life in the United States was bigger, louder, and a hundred times more peaceful than her old life in Iraq was. She was able to go to school freely, wear what she wanted, write what she wanted, and could *go* anywhere she wanted. She'd never felt so free. While she missed her parents fiercely and there were days she missed her culture, the good things about living in the US heavily outweighed the life she used to have.

And Tex and Melody were more like friends than parents, encouraging her to explore and learn. Amazingly, they even let her name their daughter, and her half-sister.

Akilah called her Alam...which meant hope in Arabic.

"Can I sit here?" a deep voice said from above her.

Akilah looked up into the man called Fish's tired, drawn face. She nodded immediately. She'd been immensely curious about him from the first moment she'd seen him...and his prosthetic. She'd met a few people in the hospitals who had prosthetic limbs, but no one who looked as unhappy about it as Fish did.

Fish sat heavily in the chair and took a long pull of the beer in his hand, but didn't speak.

Akilah wanted to talk, but was nervous about her English. She was getting much better at it, but sometimes people still had a hard time understanding her because of her accent and at times she messed up words. But because she was so curious about the man, she decided to give it a shot.

"You have new arm but do not like," she stated bluntly.

Fish turned his head and stared at her for a long

moment, before shrugging then saying, "I hate it."

Akilah reached her free arm toward him, touching the hook-like prongs with her fingertips. "Why no real hand?"

"Why don't I have one of those fancy-ass contraptions that make me look as normal as possible so people won't stare at me in disgust?" he asked.

Akilah didn't understand some of the words he used, but she got the gist of what he was saying, so she nodded.

He sighed and ran his real hand through his hair. He gazed at the lawn unseeingly, then turned and looked at her own prosthetic. Hope was sleeping peacefully in the crook of her arm and the fake hand was resting under the baby's legs.

Fish said softly, "I'm tired, Akilah. Tired of the pain. Of the pitying looks. Of missing my friends and wishing I'd been killed right alongside them."

"My parents killed in front of me," Akilah told him. "Friends shot. Raped. I felt like you. I was scared when I came to US. I could not talk or understand. But Tex and Melody took me. Loved me. They did not care about my arm. You will find this."

Fish looked at her and didn't drop his gaze. The pain and despair in his eyes clear to see. So she continued. "Someday you go where the land feeds your," she paused, searching for the right word, "inside. When your inside calms, you will find a woman. Someone who doesn't see what is missing." She glanced down at his prosthetic, then back into his eyes. "But who sees *you.*"

"I miss the mountains," Fish said, not commenting on the woman thing. "The trees. I've found that I don't like being around people anymore. Even being here today is hard."

"Then you go." Akilah shrugged and told him matter-of-factly. "When arm no hurt no more. And you are better. Find the mountains and trees. You heal."

Dane Munroe reached over and gently put his hand on the back of Akilah's neck and pulled her into him, careful not to wake baby Hope, and kissed her forehead, then sat back.

Looking into her eyes, he said with more feeling than in anything she'd heard him say all day, "Thank you."

"You're welcome," Akilah said softly, pleased to see some of the despair was gone from the man's face and the pain in his eyes had lessened.

WOLF, ABE, COOKIE, Mozart, Dude, and Benny stood in a huddle, chatting.

"You guys hear about that SEAL team we met while in Turkey looking for Tiger?" Wolf asked, sipping his beer.

"No, what about them?" Cookie asked.

"Looks like they're being reassigned to San Diego."

"No shit?" Abe asked incredously.

"No shit," Wolf confirmed.

"All of them?" Benny inquired.

Wolf nodded. "All but Ho Chi Minh. He was wounded on a mission and retired early. Married his girlfriend and I heard they moved to Belize."

"Damn," Dude breathed. "I'm sorry to hear that. That he was injured, not that he got married and is living in fucking paradise."

The guys all grinned, thinking about their own families.

"Rocco, Gumby, Ace, Bubba, Rex, and the new guy, Phantom, will be in Riverton next week. They're meeting with Commander Hurt. They only agreed on the move if they could stay together as a team. We probably won't be going on missions with them, but they were damn good to work with in Turkey. You guys want to set up a meet with them?" Wolf asked his team.

"Fuck yeah," Abe responded.

"Yes!" Benny and Mozart said at the same time.

"Sure," Cookie told Wolf.

"Definitely," Dude drawled after the others had spoken. "Anyone we can get to help look after our families while we're on missions is good for me. And of course, if they have women, we'll do the same for them."

"From what I understand, they're all single...and have vowed to stay that way," Wolf said with a grin.

"Famous last words," Benny drawled. "I should know. I said it often enough after you guys started hooking up."

Everyone chuckled. It was true. Women hadn't ever seemed to be all that important until they'd found the women meant to be theirs.

"Look at Fletch, Ghost, and Coach," Mozart said. "They were just as adamant that they'd never settle down, but they obviously changed their attitudes when they met their women."

All the SEALs nodded, knowing exactly how the Delta Force men felt.

"You guys ever think about retiring?" Cookie asked, seemingly out of the blue.

His teammates didn't respond right away, just merely looked at Cookie with intense gazes. He expanded on his seemingly blasphemous words. "I'm not saying today, but Benny, you keep popping kids out the way you are and Jessyka is going to need more help than just the temporary nanny you've got now.

And Abe, you have your hands full with your two girls, and now Tommy, and I'd bet with her huge heart, Alabama isn't done taking in foster kids. And even though Fiona has mostly put what happened behind her, I still find myself worrying about her every time I leave home. I can't get what happened years ago out of my head when she had that flashback and we were in some fucking foreign country and I couldn't get to her. I can't stand the thought of something happening to us like it did to Fish's team and leaving our families behind."

Everyone was silent, horrified at the thought of dying while on a mission, but having the possibility all too fresh in their minds after hearing about Fish's team and the last mission they were on, when Fish was injured. The man wasn't dealing very well with losing his team, feeling as if he should've done more to protect them. He'd attended each and every funeral of his teammates and had dealt with the varying accusatory and pain-filled glances their relatives had lobbed his way.

"I actually had this conversation with Caroline the other day," Wolf admitted softly, but didn't say anything else for a long moment. Everyone waited for him to continue as he gathered his thoughts.

"Tex called and told me about Fish. I came out here to Texas to see him and let him know that there were people who cared about him. It was when I got back to California that Ice brought it up. I guess I was quiet and she asked what was wrong. I told her what I could about Fish's situation. She asked if I ever thought about retiring. The thought horrified me at the time, but you're right, Cookie. I think the time is coming where I'd be satisfied being on the training side of things rather than actively going on missions."

"You think the commander would go for that?" Abe asked quietly.

Wolf shrugged. "I don't know why not. I mean, look at Rocco's team. There will *always* be teams ready to take our places. We're not getting any younger. And if we can help the up-and-coming SEALs know exactly what to expect when they're in the field, we can continue to serve our country—and be home with our families every night."

Every one of the five other men nodded introspectively.

"I'm not saying I'm ready to quit today," Dude said softly. "But I can certainly see the merits of being home with Shy every night."

Everyone chuckled. They were more than aware of Dude's sexual preferences and appetites.

The SEALs' heads all turned as a cheer went up from a group of Emily's friends who worked with her at the PX. They were drinking and laughing together and generally having a good time.

"How about this?" Wolf began, looking at his teammates, the men who were as close to him as brothers, in the eyes. "We think about it, mutually decide when the time is right, and I'll bring the idea to the commander. Let him mull it over. We're all in this together, or it won't work. We either all retire, or none of us do. Right?"

"Absolutely," Cookie said. "I *could* do it, but I don't *want* to work with another team. I trust you guys explicitly. If one of us goes, we all go. Deal?"

"Deal," all the other men agreed immediately.

PENELOPE WATCHED AS Tex kissed his wife after a song ended, and headed her way. She held her breath. She'd never met the elusive Tex, but she'd wanted to for a very long time. She knew he was the man she had to thank for helping get both Special Forces teams at the wedding over to Turkey to rescue her.

"Hi, Tiger...can we talk for a second?" Tex drawled in his distinctive southern accent.

"We're done with her," Rayne chirped. "She's all yours."

Penelope rolled her eyes at her friend and nodded at Tex. "I'd like that."

She wandered off at the former SEAL's side to a bench at the edge of the lawn.

The white lights strung around the yard twinkled and the pockets of happily laughing people made her smile. The reception was perfect. Low-key, festive, and relaxed. It was just what the men and women who sometimes struggled in big crowds needed.

She sat on the bench and waited for Tex to do the same. As soon as he was seated, Penelope said, "Thank you, Tex. I never really got a chance to say it in person. But from the bottom of my heart, thank you."

"You don't have to thank me," Tex replied immediately.

Penelope rolled her eyes. "I knew you were going to say that. And yes, I do."

"Then you're welcome," he said with a smile. "Now that we have that out of the way…how are you?"

"Good," she said immediately.

Tex eyed her closely, then asked again, "No, Tiger. How. Are. You?"

She sighed and fingered the Maltese Cross on the chain around her neck without thought. She'd worn it every day since Wolf had slipped it in her pocket at the funeral of one of the pilots who had died trying to get her out of Turkey. "I'm okay." She held up her hand when Tex opened his mouth to call her on her bullshit. "Better some days than others, but I'm getting there."

"You still seeing the therapist on base here at Fort Hood?"

She should've been surprised that Tex knew about that, but somehow she wasn't. "Yeah. When I can get up here."

"Make the effort, Tiger. There's nothing wrong with talking to someone about what you went through. As much as it sucks, I can't help you with that. Neither can any of the Deltas. They can commiserate, and empathize, but they don't *know*."

The tears that seemed to always be waiting at the surface filled her eyes and Penelope looked away, trying to control herself. The twinkling lights blurred as she stared sightlessly at them.

She felt a warm hand rest on her knee. "I'm not saying that to be a dick, only to tell you to give yourself some slack. What's your biggest fear?"

Penelope looked at Tex in confusion. "What?"

"Your biggest fear in regards to what happened. What is it?"

Penelope shook her head. "It's stupid."

"It's not. What is it?"

"There are two," she whispered, as if saying them out loud would make them come true right that moment. "The dark…and being lost and no one can find me…again."

Tex's hand closed around her own, making her realize how hard she was squeezing the cross around her neck. Penelope could feel the pendant lightly digging into her skin as he spoke. "As far as the second fear goes, you don't *ever* have to worry about being lost, Tiger. I got your back."

She looked into the depths of Tex's eyes and saw nothing but sincerity there. She hadn't met this man before, but she trusted him. And she knew exactly what he meant. She'd known it the minute she'd pulled the necklace out of her pocket and realized what the note from Wolf's wife meant.

Our men rescued us, and since they rescued you too, you're now one of us.

Wear this and you'll never be lost again.

A tracker. The pendant concealed a miniature tracker inside. It could've been creepy, but instead it was comforting. No matter where she went, Tex would know. He could send someone to find her. The safety net was a huge relief. The tears she'd been holding back spilled over. "Thank you."

"You're welcome," Tex repeated. He let go of her hand and sat back. "Now, about that first fear. There's not much I can do about that, but I expect the large guy glaring at me from across the way can." He motioned to the other side of the lawn with his chin.

Penelope wiped the tears from her face and looked over to where Tex had indicated. Moose stood there with his arms across his chest, his feet planted wide, glaring at Tex as if he wanted to beat the shit out of him for making her cry. The corner of her mouth twitched up.

"That's just Moose."

"Yeah, and if you gave him a chance, 'Just Moose' would slay all your dragons and keep you from worrying about the dark every night as you slept in his arms."

Penelope looked at Tex in surprise. "You're really blunt."

The other man shrugged. "Why shouldn't I be? Life is too damn short to go through it walking on eggshells. From the moment I first talked to Melody online, I knew I wanted to be the one by her side and protect her from harm."

"Isn't that a bit sexist?" Penelope bit out, harsher than she meant it to sound. "I don't need to be protected and coddled."

Tex didn't look put out in the least. He merely shrugged. "Maybe. Maybe not. But I'll be the first person to tell you that my Melody can take care of herself. She's tough, smart, and a bit of a badass. But, that doesn't mean that I still don't want to protect her.

And it also doesn't mean that at night, when she's had a tough day, she's tired from work and nursing our daughter, that she doesn't let me coddle and take care of her. And it feels damn good. For both of us."

"I can take care of myself," Penelope said softly.

"Of course you can," Tex returned without hesitation. "You're a capable adult who has lived on her own for years, who rescues people from burning buildings and crumpled cars, who survived three months in captivity at the hands of ISIS, who's the American Princess…but that doesn't mean you can't let someone else, someone who desperately wants to shield you from the shit life can throw at you, stand at your side, your back, and even in front of you from time to time."

Penelope let Tex's words sink in, then said softly, "I shouldn't be scared of the dark. It's childish and stupid."

"It's not," Tex retorted immediately. "You went through hell, Tiger," Tex said just as quietly. "I'm not surprised you've got some tics. But honey, if being scared of the dark is the biggest thing you're struggling with, you're stronger than I ever imagined."

Penelope looked up at the man who literally saved her life without even knowing her. He'd convinced the powers that be to send in the SEALs after her. When they'd all disappeared after their plane had crashed, he'd been the one to use the trackers to find them and send in the Deltas to scoop them up and get them to safety.

He was right. Absolutely right. So what if she was scared of the dark? She was a badass motherfuck-er...who needed a nightlight. So what?

"You're right," she said finally.

"I know," was his response.

"I know who you are, and I'm trying to be okay with you touching Pen and making her cry, but I swear to God, if she doesn't smile in the next five seconds, me and you are gonna have words."

Moose's words were low and threatening, and Penelope couldn't help the shiver that ran through her. She'd known Moose liked her, but seeing him openly get pissed off and defensive on her behalf was a new thing.

Tex didn't even flinch. He merely stood and gestured to his seat. "She's all yours, Tucker," then walked off, whistling.

Moose looked after him with a frown on his face, then looked back down at Penelope. "He's a bit spooky."

"You don't know the half of it. Sit, Moose. Keep me company."

He did, and as if he hadn't practically beat his chest Tarzan-style at the thought of Tex upsetting her,

Moose chatted about nothing in particular. Giving her the space she still needed, even though she knew he didn't want to.

Penelope didn't know if she'd ever be in a position to open herself up to Moose, to be more than friends, but she was grateful that at the moment, he wasn't giving up on her.

"COME 'ERE, LOVE," Fletch said, pulling Emily against him. He settled her back against his chest and wrapped his arms around her belly. Resting his cheek against hers, he looked out at the guests still at the reception.

They'd cut the cake, had their first dance and suffered through his friends giving cheesy and corny toasts. His parents had left thirty minutes ago. Fletch could tell they were exhausted; the medical issues his mom had still causing her problems. He hated to see them getting older, but was happy as he could be they'd made it to his wedding.

They'd loved Annie on sight, and loved that she'd immediately started calling them Nana and Papa. The little girl had entertained them most of the evening by regaling them with tales from her school, about her favorite PE teacher, the cute first grade teacher in her school who wore ties with cartoon characters on them, about her favorite obstacle courses, how Truck had bought combat boots for her, and endless other stories about his teammates.

His daughter was now sitting off to the side talking with Akilah, not caring that the teenager probably didn't understand half of what she said because she was talking so quickly. Annie loved everyone. She was a lovely child who was a bit quirky, but people were drawn to her.

As if she could read his mind, Emily said quietly, "Did you see Annie talking to your new friend, Dane, tonight?"

Fletch nodded. "Yeah. She was amazing with him."

Emily chuckled. "If you call asking him a million questions about his arm and how he lost it and how his prosthetic worked amazing."

"Yeah, that's what I meant," Fletch agreed immediately. "I know it might've seemed obtrusive, but it wasn't. He needs to talk about it. And Annie sensed that. I watched as she listened intently to him telling her that his friends and teammates died. And when she reached up and put her cheek against his and hugged him…he almost lost it."

Emily nodded. "I swear to God, I have no idea how she's become as amazing as she has. I'm in awe of her."

"It's because she has the most amazing mother," Fletch told her without missing a beat. "A lot of single mothers get caught up in chasing the next dollar, or keeping their head above water. But you? You didn't. Everything you did was for her. From her schools, to making sure she had the right nutrition, and staying up late and reading to her when she was little. *You* are why she's as amazing as she is."

Emily turned in Fletch's arms and looked up at him. "I love you, Cormac Fletcher."

"And I love *you*, Emily Fletcher," he returned immediately.

She looked around. "It was a good party, wasn't it?"

"Definitely. I've enjoyed getting to know the SEALs better. And having TJ, Penelope, Fish, and even Tex here was just icing on the cake. Did your friends from the PX have a good time?"

Emily laughed and gestured to where the group was still laughing and talking. "I think they've drunk more than your military friends. So yeah, they're having a good time."

"Good," Fletch answered immediately, pulling her closer into him. He could feel his body reacting to her nearness. He openly gazed down at her breasts, trying to look down her shirt.

She laughed and slapped a hand over her chest,

cutting off his view.

"Hey," he mock complained, "those are my tits now."

Emily rolled her eyes. "As if."

Fletch leaned down and nuzzled the side of her neck, then took her earlobe into his mouth and bit down gently. He whispered, "When can we kick everyone out?"

He felt Emily's laugh against him more than he heard it. "Not yet. You need to be patient. Taking me against the wall should've tided you over."

"I'll never get enough of you, love. Never. You should know, I'm going to be one of those guys who has a prescription for Viagra so even when I'm eighty-five, I can still make love to my wife."

Emily looked at him with a weird expression on her face then finally said, "I don't know whether to be disgusted by that, or to think it's the most romantic thing I've ever heard."

Fletch shrugged. "Don't care. It is what it is. Did Mary say anything?"

Knowing he was talking about what they'd done in the other woman's apartment, Emily nodded. "Of course she did. You know her. The first chance she got, she cornered me and demanded to know where we did it and if she needed to wash her sheets, couch, or table."

Fletch chuckled. "What'd you tell her?"

Emily blushed, but said, "That she didn't need to wash anything, that we managed not to have sex on any surface of her house that she had to eat, cook, sit, or sleep on. I have no idea how she figured it out, but she immediately said, 'Wall sex. Awesome.' Then she gave me an approving look, and walked away." Emily shook her head. "It was almost spooky how she figured it out so fast."

"I hate to tell you this," Fletch told his wife, tightening his arms around her before continuing. "But Mary called me two nights ago and threatened my life if I took you on any of the furniture in her house. She said she loved us both, but she drew the line at bodily fluids contaminating her stuff. I asked if her walls were off-limits, and she laughed and said no. As long as no bare skin touched her stuff, we could do whatever we wanted."

Emily giggled and shook her head. "We have awesome friends."

"That we do," Fletch agreed. Then he kissed her. Long, slow, and deep. Showing her without words how happy he was and how proud he was to make her his wife.

Suddenly, without warning, a harsh voice rang out over the soft music playing and the chatter of the guests.

"Nobody move or you're all fucking dead! Do as we say and no one will get hurt."

Fletch's head whipped up—and he stared incredously at the four men standing around the yard, each had a bandana over their faces and an AK-47 in their hands, pointed at the guests.

Fuckin' A. They were supposed to be the best trained soldiers in the world. How in the world had these assholes snuck up on them? They'd let their guard down, been distracted by the reception and had gotten complacent.

As soon as the thought, *who the fuck would be dumb enough to rob a party with the most badass soldiers on the planet in attendance,* ran through his mind, Fletch heard his daughter exclaim, "Oh goody! Now Daddy Fletch can kick some ass!"

Chapter Four

THE MAN WHO had spoken the threat gestured with his rifle. "Women and kids over there, men over there."

Fletch felt Emily tense in his arms and her head immediately turned to look for Annie. He liked that her first concern was always for her daughter. When they had children together, she'd be the best mother. He just had to convince her that sooner rather than later was good. After he got rid of these fuckers trying to ruin his reception.

"Now, assholes!" the man barked.

Fletch let go of Emily and lightly pushed her toward Annie. "Go on, love. Stay calm, this'll be over before you know it."

She didn't speak, merely nodded before squeezing his arm tightly once, her nails digging into his skin, before walking toward her daughter without looking back.

Fletch immediately moved to the area where the gunman indicated the men should congregate. He and his teammates gathered together to one side of the group of men. Watching. Waiting.

He noted that Wolf and his SEAL teammates had done the same thing. The Special Forces operatives were on either side of the group of men, the PX employees and some of the civilian contractors from Fort Hood stood in the middle.

Three of the gunmen came over to where the men were standing and stood guard around them. Each had a finger on the triggers of their rifles and looked more than ready to shoot at the slightest provocation.

"Here's the deal. No one will get hurt if you follow our directions to the letter. We're not fucking around. One by one, come forward and put your watches here," he pointed to the table about five feet off to the side. "Your wallets, phones, and any other jewelry you're wearing as well." He paused and pointed to Fletch specifically. "Wedding rings too. All of it. If you try to hide anything, I'll shoot one of the women. If I see anyone with a phone in their hand trying to call nine-one-one, I'll shoot you on sight. Don't be a hero and you'll live."

Fletch ground his teeth together. There was nothing he and his fellow soldiers hated more than someone threatening women and children. Bastards.

Slowly the men around him began to do as the man demanded, removing their wallets from their pockets and taking off any jewelry they were wearing.

As the gunmen were distracted by the guests coming forward one by one, Fletch murmured, "Plan?" to Ghost.

Ghost and the other Deltas were waiting their turn to place their belongings on the table and sizing up the situation. One glance over at the SEALs showed they were doing the same thing.

"For now, we wait," Ghost replied.

"These assholes are not going to crash my wedding reception and rob everyone," Fletch said, pissed way the hell off.

"If it was just us, we could rush them," Ghost said calmly, "but it's not. Look." He gestured to the women with an almost imperceptible jerk of his head.

Fletch looked over to where the women were standing and every muscle in his body locked. The fourth gunman was standing behind Annie and had one hand resting on her shoulder, holding her tightly. The other still held the rifle, and his finger was on the fucking trigger. He was standing sideways, so he could see both the women he was guarding and the men on the other side of the yard.

"Easy, Fletch," Coach warned from his other side. "She's okay for now."

"For now," Fletch ground out. "If one hair on my daughter's head is damaged, I'll fucking kill him."

"We all will," Truck agreed.

"Shut the fuck up," one of other gunmen ordered, speaking up for the first time. He had a heavy southern accent and his voice was deeper than the original man's tone. "You, get your ass over here, and put your shit on the table" he ordered, gesturing at Fletch.

Wanting to rip the rifle out of the man's hands more than he wanted anything else in his life, Fletch took a deep breath and obediently walked over to where the other men had begun to pile their belongings. He laid his wallet on the table, then slowly, ever so slowly, removed his watch. Then, without losing eye contact with the man, telling him without words he was going to regret picking his party, his house, and his friends to rob, Fletch tugged off the wedding ring Emily had placed on his finger hours before. The ring he'd sworn never to remove unless it was absolutely necessary during his top secret missions. He placed it carefully on top of his wallet, then backed up.

"That all?" the man with the rifle asked snidely.

Fletch held his arms out to his sides and answered in a quiet and deadly voice, "You want to frisk me to check?"

The man hesitated for a fraction of a second before sneering, "If I find out you're holding back, you'll regret it."

"It's *you* who will regret this night," Fletch told

him in a low, even voice, standing stock still but vibrating with an intense kind of anticipation. The type he only got right before a mission. Right before the shit hit the fan and they had to kill or be killed.

They had threated his woman. His child. They would *not* be leaving his property uninjured...or at all. He had no worries about anyone going to jail if the men were killed, the cameras on his property would back up the fact that they'd acted in self-defense.

"Get the fuck back over there, big man," the guy with the rifle finally ordered, gesturing back to the group of men.

Without a word, Fletch did as he was ordered, his arms still out at his sides, not taking his eyes from the man as he walked backward toward Ghost and the rest of his team.

One by one, the other men in the group walked forward and emptied their pockets, put their precious wedding rings on the ever-growing pile of valuables, visibly hating every second of staring down the barrels of the weapons.

When it was Tex's turn to give up his valuables, the former SEAL limped up to the table.

Fletch's facial expression didn't change, but since he'd never seen Tex limp in his life, it was obvious, at least to the soldiers in the group, that he was faking an injury. The only question was why and what he had planned.

"You some sort of cripple?" the man with the southern accent jeered.

"Missing part of my leg," Tex admitted in a high-pitched voice.

"Let me see," the first gunman demanded from off to the side.

Without hesitation, Tex lifted his pant leg and showed off the prosthetic he was wearing. It was one of his metallic ones, not a realistic flesh-colored one. The gunman had the audacity to walk up to him and tap the butt of the rifle against the metal, the resulting sound ugly and harsh in the night air. "How much that cost?" he asked, the greed easy to read in his eyes and tone.

"Please, I can't afford to replace it," Tex whined, indicating without saying exactly that it was worth a lot of money.

"Take it off," the first man demanded.

"But I can't walk without it," Tex complained.

"Do I look like I give a shit?" the gunman asked rhetorically. "Take it off. Add it to the pile. You can crawl your ass back to the others for all I care."

"I'll need help walking," Tex replied.

The third guy guarding the men spoke up for the first time. "You, come help him," he ordered.

Fletch looked over to see who the man had indicated and barely held back a grin as Fish took a step forward. He wasn't sure what Tex had planned, but he'd bet his house and everything in it this was exactly what Tex wanted.

"Looks like you're a crip too. Take off your fake arm," the gunman told Fish. "We've got a group of crippled motherfuckers here."

Keeping his eyes to the ground, Fish didn't say a word, merely walked forward to where Tex was standing and stopped when he was shoulder to shoulder with the other man. Still without words, Tex helped Fish unstrap and remove his shoulder harness and take off his prosthetic. Fish added his wallet and watch to the table, then put his good arm around Tex's waist and assisted him back to the group of men.

Fletch smiled grimly. Fish was pissed. The anger and hostility was coming off the man in waves. He'd put money on both Tex and Fish any day of the week over the assholes with the weapons. It didn't matter that Tex only had one leg and Fish one arm. They could take any one of the men down, but they all needed to bide their time. Wait until the right moment to act. The more the gunmen underestimated the group, the sooner the operatives, past and present, could make their move.

And there was no doubt a move would be made. The SEALs were standing at the other end of the group of men. They seemed as if they were relaxed, but Fletch knew by looking at them they were ready to pounce. Wolf's hands were moving in a way Fletch knew he was communicating with his men. Signaling. And the others were communicating back to Wolf. Whatever happened, they'd move as one.

Fletch's own teammates were standing the same way. Loose and ready. They didn't have a secret way of talking to each other, but they'd worked together for so long and had trained for this kind of situation enough, they all had plan A, B, C, D, and probably E and F already down pat, and could switch from one to the other within seconds.

TJ, the former Delta sniper, was standing in the middle of the group of men, his arms crossed over his chest, not hiding the pissed-off, you-don't-scare-me look on his face.

Different scenarios ran through Fletch's head. The three men guarding them were spaced evenly apart. The table of their belongings was in the middle, the man with a southern accent guarding it. TJ, Tex, and Fish could take him out. The man who'd first ordered them to separate from the women was standing near the Delta team, and the third man was on the side with the SEALs.

If it was only them, without the civilians and women in attendance, the men would already have the assholes disarmed and laying on the ground, wishing they'd passed by this house and this party. But it *wasn't* only them. The last man was with the women. And while Fletch knew his wife was brave, as was Mary, Rayne, Harley, and probably the other women too, they weren't soldiers.

But Penelope was.

Fletch took his eyes off Annie as she stood in the grasp of the last gunman and found the Army Princess. She was looking at him as if her life depended on it. Not at Annie. Not at the gunman. At *him*.

They stared at each other from across the lawn for a long moment. Then Penelope gave a tiny chin lift, acknowledging him and his team. Then she brought her hand up to her chest and laid her palm over her heart and nodded in the direction of the man essentially holding Annie hostage.

Fletch didn't like it. He really didn't, but if Penelope could handle the gunman on her side of the yard, his team, and the SEALs, could handle the three on their side. He didn't particularly like not being able to take out that fourth man himself, but he was too far away…and Penelope was a trained soldier.

"No," Moose ground out from next to him.

Fletch shuffled until his body was turned toward the firefighter and moved his eyes, not his head, to look at the man.

He was pissed. And his eyes were glued to Penelope's. He'd seen the nonverbal signals she'd sent to Fletch and wasn't happy about it. Way not happy.

"It'll work," Fletch said tonelessly.

"She's too small," Moose argued.

Fletch had concerns about that himself. Tiger's five feet two inches weren't ideal to try to take down the six-foot-plus man threatening Annie and the rest of the women. But instead of arguing about it, he said, "Have her six."

It was a military term which meant to have someone's back. Fletch had no idea if the firefighter understood or not, but it wasn't as if he could have an in-depth conversation with the twitchy-fingered thugs nearby.

Moose's jaw flexed as he ground his teeth together, but he nodded once.

Fletch sighed silently in relief. He'd understood.

It was tricky. Penelope was all the way across the yard and they'd only have seconds to all work together, but it would happen.

The only wildcard in the plan was Annie.

Chapter Five

EMILY WAS PISSED. This was her wedding reception. It was supposed to be a fun time. A time to celebrate new beginnings with her husband and hang out with their friends. And it *had* been fun. Lots of fun. Until these assholes decided to take what didn't belong to them. And to threaten them.

She glared at the man holding her daughter against him with all the hatred she'd had no idea she had in her heart.

"Easy, Em," Rayne said in a quiet voice. "Don't do anything rash."

"If he hurts her in any way, I'll kill him," Emily replied.

"You won't have to, because Fletch will get there first," her friend returned immediately.

"Shut up," the man holding her daughter said sharply. "No talking."

They stood silent, watching as the men across the yard came forward one by one and laid their belongings on a table in front of one of the men holding a rifle. Emily stood in front of the group of women, Rayne on her left and Harley on her right. Mary was standing next to Rayne and Penelope was on the other side next to Harley. They were all standing in a row in front of Melody, baby Hope, and Akilah. Shielding them, keeping the gunmen from getting their hands on any other children to use as hostages.

Emily watched as Fletch came forward to drop his wallet on the table, and she flinched as he slowly took off his wedding ring. She wasn't an idiot, she knew he'd need to remove it when he went on a mission for his safety, but seeing him take off the symbol of their love hours after she'd slipped it on his finger hurt. A lot.

But it was obvious he was just as unhappy with the situation. Emily watched as her husband held his arms out from his sides aggressively, as if he was goading the gunman to hurt him. She held her breath. After a few words, Fletch backed away, his arms still out, until he was back amongst the group of men. She blew out a relieved breath.

"Looks like your lover's cooperating, little bride. Smart."

Emily glared at the gunman. It was obvious they'd scoped out the reception before making their move. She and Fletch had cut the small wedding cake they'd ordered and had their first dance together, as all couples did. If this guy knew she was the bride, then they'd probably known about the reception before tonight. It couldn't have been random. Fletch's house wasn't exactly on a main road. She wondered how many other parties and receptions they'd done this at. Fuckers.

Annie took a deep breath, as if she was going to mouth off to the man with his hand on her shoulder, but Penelope spoke up before she could. "You're scaring that little girl," she announced in a voice loud enough for the gunman to hear her, but not the others across the yard.

"Do I look like I care?" the man drawled, tightening his grip on Annie's shoulders.

"If you make her cry, it's just going to piss off her daddy," Penelope told him.

Emily looked over at the other woman, not sure why she was saying that. Then she looked back at her daughter. Annie didn't look scared at all. She looked angry. She had a look on her face that Emily imagined was mirrored on her own.

Annie's eyes went from Penelope to her mom, then back to Penelope.

"She's almost shaking, she's so scared," Penelope enunciated carefully.

At her words, Annie sniffed loudly and Emily could see her small body begin to shake.

Emily narrowed her eyes and tried to read her daughter. She'd never seen her shake like that when she'd cried before. In fact, Annie wasn't really a crier. She was tough and could usually shake off her tears when she got hurt. Before she could examine the situation further and see if Annie really was hurt in some way, and if she needed to take action, Melody gasped from behind her and whispered, "John!"

Emily's eyes whipped up to the group of men and saw Melody's husband limping badly; it was obviously his turn to approach the table and hand over his valuables.

"What in the world?" Melody said under her breath as they all watched the strong and capable former SEAL speak with the gunman. His shoulders were hunched and his head was down. They couldn't hear what was being said, but within moments, Fish sauntered up to Tex.

In contrast to the SEAL, Fish didn't look cowed at all. He kept his eyes glued to the man with the gun as they spoke. Then, almost in tandem, the two men removed their prosthetics and added them to the growing pile on the table. Fish then helped Tex back to the group.

"Tex hurt?" Akilah asked her mother softly.

"No," Melody whispered. "It's a plan. Your dad is just as strong with one leg."

"Like Baby," Akilah said, the relief easy to hear in her voice.

"Exactly, like our dog, Baby," Melody confirmed. The coonhound only had three legs, but she got along just as well as a four-legged dog. They'd left her back home with Melody's best friend, Amy, and her family. They all loved Baby as much as Melody did…almost.

They continued to watch the men empty their pockets one by one. The testosterone emanating from across the yard was thick and dangerous. Emily had no idea how the gunmen didn't feel it. Yet she knew without a doubt they didn't, because if they had, they'd be as far away from this yard as they could get.

Emily's attention was divided between her daughter and husband, and she was almost ashamed to realize that she was looking at Fletch more than Annie. When she looked at Annie, she felt scared and powerless because she couldn't help her. But when she looked at Fletch, she felt reassured, safe, protected.

He was pissed, no doubt about it, but he was in control. He and his teammates and friends would make sure nothing happened to them. She knew they most certainly had a plan.

Fletch's eyes hadn't met hers since he'd given up his valuables, but suddenly they stopped scanning the area and locked on something to her right. Emily turned her head and saw Penelope looking intently in the direction of Fletch and the other Delta soldiers.

She watched as Penelope made several movements with her head and arms. She looked back to Fletch and saw him nod once. She had no idea what was going on, but whatever it was had something to do with Penelope. Emily hadn't really thought about it much, but realized with a start that Penelope had been a soldier too. She'd thought of her as more of a firefighter than anything else, but she didn't get the nickname The Army Princess for nothing.

"Time to get to work, girlie," the man who was holding Annie said gruffly.

The little girl looked up and over her shoulder at him, but didn't say anything.

"Your job is to go to each woman here and get all her jewelry. Earrings, necklaces, rings, bracelets…everything. Don't skip anybody, and don't let anyone keep anything." He raised his voice and told the assembled group of women, "If anyone holds anything back, *anything*, I'll hurt this little girl. You try to keep your wedding ring; I'll break one of her fingers. You hide a bracelet, I'll break her wrist. If you don't empty your pockets, I'll pull her shoulder out of its socket. And if still *more* of you stupidly hold back, I'll take that little baby you're all trying to pretend I can't see you standing in front of, and I'll snap every one of her fingers one by one then break both legs."

Emily stared at the man in shock. Up until now, he'd seemed fairly calm, especially compared to the other thugs. But he'd only been able to hide his crazy better. If he had no compunctions in hurting Annie, or breaking little Hope's legs and fingers, he wouldn't hesitate to shoot any one of them.

"No hurt Alam," Akilah said fiercely under her breath.

"It's okay," Melody told her daughter, putting a hand on her forearm both in warning and comfort.

Annie had a mutinous look on her face, but didn't say a word, nor even look at the man who'd just threatened to hurt her in awful ways. She marched to her left and stood in front of one of Emily's friends from the PX. She held out her little hand and the woman took off her earrings, then watch, then the sweet pearl necklace she had on. She placed them all in Annie's cupped hands and, without a word, not asking if the woman was sure that was all she had, Annie turned around and went back to the man with her head down.

She held them out to him and he looked around as if trying to figure out where to put the jewelry. He obviously hadn't thought this whole collecting-the-jewelry thing through. He looked at one of the older women who had a purse over her shoulder and ordered, "You. Bring your bag over here."

She did and held it out to him.

He didn't even reach for it, and instead told Annie, "Take it around with you from person to person and put everything in there."

Without a word, Annie took the leather bag from the woman and dropped the jewelry from the first woman inside. Then she turned and went back to where she'd started and stood in front of the second woman.

Person by person, Annie continued through the group, not saying anything, just adding to the stash of jewels inside the bag.

When she got to Penelope, Annie looked straight into the woman's eyes as Penelope spoke. "You're a brave kid, Annie. Thank you. You haven't even cried, even though I know you probably want to. It's okay, you know. *It's okay to cry.*"

Annie nodded, then finally spoke for the first time. "I'm so scared," she said loudly. "I don't want my fingers broken."

"Of course you don't," Penelope soothed. "But everyone is going to give you all their jewelry, so you won't need to worry about it." She reached behind her neck and unclasped her necklace. Emily was watching the other woman intently, feeling as if she was missing something. Something her daughter was reading loud and clear.

Penelope looked calm and in control, and Emily would've missed the small sign she wasn't as calm as she was pretending to be if she hadn't been watching Penelope so carefully. Right before she dropped her necklace into the bag Annie was holding out, she hesitated and her thumb rubbed over the Maltese cross in a wistful caress.

"That's right," Harley chimed in. "We're giving you all we have so no one will get hurt."

Emily kept her eyes glued to her daughter. She'd said she was scared, but her voice didn't really *sound* scared. Annie was now nodding at Penelope and Emily's eyes whipped up to the firefighter's face. She'd missed whatever the woman had whispered to her daughter, but Penelope was now giving Annie a small smile.

"All right, enough with the chitchat!" the man with the gun barked. "Hurry up, girlie. Stop dawdling."

Annie nodded and moved to stand in front of Harley. The woman took off all her jewelry and then put her hand reassuredly on Annie's shoulder.

Then Annie was standing in front of her mom.

Emily took in a shuddering breath and looked down at her daughter sadly. She removed her necklace and dropped it onto the other pieces of jewelry. She removed one earring, then the next. She slowly removed the two bracelets on her wrists, both of which had been gifts from Fletch. Finally, she reached for her wedding rings.

"It's okay, Mommy," Annie said so softly Emily knew no one but her and maybe Rayne and Harley could hear her. "Daddy Fletch won't let anyone take your special rings away. And soldier Annie is on the job."

There wasn't an ounce of fear or doubt on her little girl's face, which scared the shit out of Emily. "Let Daddy handle this," she ordered her daughter, regretting letting her play soldier with Fletch's friends for the first time. She didn't want Annie to think she could do anything in this situation. She was just a little girl. *Not* a soldier, as much as she wanted to be one.

"No one is handling this," the gunman boomed, obviously having overheard her not-quite-whispered, panicked words to her daughter. "No one but us, that is. Now hurry the fuck up, girlie. I'm getting impatient."

As if his words flicked a switch inside her head, Annie whimpered and turned to face him as she said, "Don't hurt me, please. I'm doing the best I can. This bag is really really heavy."

"Whatever," the man grumbled. "Just get it done."

Annie nodded and stepped to Rayne. Her eyes came back up to Emily's and she winked. *Winked.*

Emily realized in that moment that Annie *did* think she was in another adventure. It wasn't bad enough that her elementary school had been on lockdown because of a madman who'd entered with a gun, and Annie and her classmates had to climb out the windows of their classroom to escape. It wasn't bad enough that someone had drugged her and she'd had to dig her way out of a big metal container to escape. No, now Annie was smack dab in the middle of a robbery at her own mom and dad's wedding reception.

She opened her mouth to snap at her daughter. To tell her that this wasn't a game and that she could get seriously hurt, but Akilah's halting English words stopped her.

"I have arm. You want that too?"

"What?" the man barked, confused either by what she'd said, or because he didn't understand her because of her thick accent.

"My arm. You want? The others gave theirs." The teenager pointed at the table across the way in front of the men.

The man with the gun turned to look across the yard at his comrades, saw the prosthetic arm and leg sitting on the table with the men's belongings, then turned back to the Iraqi girl. "Yeah. Take the fucking thing off. Looks like we have quite the collection of limbs to take with us today." Then he laughed maniacally.

As Annie continued taking the rest of the women's jewelry, Akilah removed her prosthetic. It was quite a bit more sophisticated than Fish's. It had Akilah's same skin tone and a hand and fingers at the end instead of a simple three-pronged hook as the former Delta's had.

Emily thought morbidly that if the girl put fake blood on the end, it would look exactly like a real arm that had been cut off someone's body. It was a weird thought, but this was a weird situation.

Annie finally got around to Akilah and Melody. She lifted the purse over her head so it was hanging across her small body and reached her arms out for the prosthetic.

"I'll be careful," Annie promised softly.

"It's heavy," Akilah told Annie in a low voice.

Annie didn't say anything, but Emily saw her nod slightly to herself as she hefted the prosthetic.

"Get over here!" the man ordered harshly. "Stop talking! Jesus! How many times do I have to fucking say it?"

Annie's shoulders slumped and she limped back up to where the man was standing, as if the bag across her body was simply too heavy for her to comfortably carry. When she got within touching distance, the man grabbed her shoulder once more and hauled her in front of him again. Annie held on to Akilah's arm by clasping it to the front of her little body and wrapping her arms around it, as if it was a prized teddy bear instead of an arm.

"You got all the stuff?" one of the men holding the rifles on the male guests shouted across the yard.

"Yeah!"

"All of it?" the man inquired.

"I said yes," the gunman holding Annie groused. "I got it fucking all."

"Have the kid bring it over here," the other man ordered impatiently.

"You heard him, get going," their captor said, shoving Annie in the middle of her back, making her stumble and almost fall to the ground. She kept her feet, barely, and turned to the man with the gun.

"B-but I'm s-scared," Annie said, holding on to Akilah's prosthetic even harder.

"Good," he told her unfeelingly. "Then you won't do anything stupid and no one will get hurt."

Annie turned and shuffled across the grass with her head down and shoulders slumped. Emily felt her own shoulders stiffen in concern as her daughter struggled with the weight of the bag. She watched as the man across the way said something to her, then reached out and ripped the purse over her head and put one hand against her chest and pushed.

Annie fell backwards, landing on her butt in the grass. Akilah's arm, which she'd been holding onto, went flying out of her grasp and landed in the grass next to her. Then Annie opened her mouth and wailed.

Cried loud enough for baby Hope to stir and begin to fret in response to Annie's cries.

Loud enough for Emily to gasp and take a step forward, stopped by both Harley and Rayne's grips on her biceps.

Loud enough for Fletch, Truck, and Dude to also take a step forward, as if they wanted to scoop Annie up and comfort her. Luckily they stopped after one step and stayed frozen in place.

Loud enough for the man who had pushed her to lift one hand up to his ear as if shielding it from the high-pitched wails coming from the small child on the ground.

Loud enough for the man who had been guarding the women to throw back his head and laugh in glee at the tortured sounds coming out of the girl he'd threatened minutes earlier.

Finally, one of the thugs across the way shouted to be heard over Annie's wails, "Shut up and go back over to the women!"

Annie either ignored him, or didn't hear, because she didn't move except to roll over, grab onto Akilah's fake arm, and hug it to her body. If anything, her cries got louder.

The man who had pushed her leaned over and hauled Annie upright by one of her arms. Annie managed to keep hold of the prosthetic and continued to cry. Emily watched, her hands clenched into fists as the man leaned into her and said something to her daughter.

Annie's cries didn't ease, but she nodded then spun and started walking back toward the women. Emily breathed out a small sigh of relief. They weren't out of danger, not by any stretch, but at least she'd have her baby closer to her. One bad guy with a gun was better than three.

Annie continued to cry as she approached the man with the gun.

"What in the hell are you crying about?" he asked impatiently.

"I f-f-fell," Annie wailed, stopping in front of him.

"And?"

"It huuuuuuurt!"

"Oh good Lord," the man muttered. "I can't believe you're being such a baby. He didn't even push you that hard. Suck it up."

Emily's blood boiled. How dare he tell her child to suck it up. He had no right. No right to belittle her pain. No right to threaten her. No right to even *be* there.

Just when Emily was about to march over to her daughter and snatch her away from the guy with the gun and comfort her, the man looked away from Annie to bellow something at his fellow robber asshole friends.

Annie's cries didn't diminish one iota but her eyes swung to Penelope, as did Emily's, as she'd been closely watching her daughter, and the firefighter/soldier nodded once.

Emily watched in horror and fear as her daughter grabbed Akilah's prosthetic arm as if she was holding a baseball bat and swung it at the man's legs as hard as she could.

Chapter Six

FLETCH'S EYES WERE on his daughter. When the man with the southern accent pushed her and she went flying and landed hard on the grass, he gasped in horror and fury.

Then when she began to squeal in pain, he took a step forward, noticing that Truck did the same. Luckily, they both stopped themselves before they rushed to Annie, but it took everything Fletch had to make himself stand still.

The man who pushed her lifted one hand to his ear to try to block the high-pitched wails coming from the child.

Fletch saw the man across the way laughing. Fletch's eyes narrowed. That would be the man to worry about. Anyone who could laugh at the sounds of anguish coming out of a child's voice had no soul.

It took a moment, but Fletch finally realized that Annie's cries were fake. She had no tears in her eyes and was moaning and screaming more than she was actually crying. Her wails had bothered him at first because she hardly ever cried, and the fact that she was now had horrified him, but finally he paid more attention and realized that the little bugger was faking it. He had no idea what she thought she was doing, but if she was trying to cause a distraction, he needed to be ready. He hated that she was putting herself in danger, but the only thing he could do at this point was make sure she stayed alive.

The men holding them hostage obviously hadn't been around kids much, if at all, because they had no inkling that Annie was faking her tantrum.

While the gunmen were distracted by her wails, Fletch leaned over to Ghost and said quietly and quickly. "Annie is purposely making a distraction. Tiger has the other guy. We'll take the tango closest to us, Fish, Tex, and TJ have the southern-talking asshole, and Ghost and his team'll take the quiet one."

"Tiger's backup?" Ghost asked urgently.

"Her man. Moose. And if I had to guess, I'd say Truck'll be over there for Mary before we blink. I wouldn't be surprised if a SEAL or two also joined in that fray. As much as I hate to admit it, Tiger'll need the help. That asshole is fucking crazy." Fletch hadn't spoken with Truck, but the other man had moved himself to the outer edge of their group, in a position where he could easily sprint to the other side of the yard in seconds.

"Ten-four."

"Can Annie handle it?" Ghost asked worriedly.

"Abso-fucking-lutely," Fletch returned. He wasn't happy about it, but he hadn't seen any terror in Annie's eyes when she'd found his in the crowd, instead seeing excitement. He wasn't sure what that meant, probably that he was a piss-poor parent, but at the moment he couldn't bring himself to care. He was too relieved that she wasn't trembling in fear and scared out of her mind. The last thing he wanted was her mom and dad's wedding day to be the reason she needed therapy for the rest of her life.

Fletch turned to Wolf and inclined his head in Annie's direction, then over at Tiger standing with the women. Wolf nodded in response and turned his eyes to the man guarding them. Satisfied that Wolf's team would take care of the threat on that side, Fletch's gaze went back to his daughter, who was still giving the performance of her life.

The man who'd pushed her finally had enough of Annie's tears, because he bellowed, "Get up and go back over to the women!"

Annie didn't respond except to roll over onto her side and clutch the prosthetic arm she'd been carrying to her chest. Without a word, the man hovering over her grabbed the little girl by her arm and hauled her to her feet, leaning in and saying something to her.

Fletch gritted his teeth. The man had better not be threatening his daughter.

Annie merely nodded, then headed back across the clearing without another look in his direction. The hair on the back of Fletch's neck stood up straight. This was it. Whatever Annie and Tiger had planned was about to go down.

He glanced at the gunmen, surprised when they looked relaxed and at ease. They thought they had the situation under control and somehow didn't feel the dangerous vibes in the air. Idiots.

Annie arrived back at the lone gunman's side over by the women and Fletch could see them talking to each other. He could still hear Annie crying as she spoke.

Then the man moved putting his back to the women. He started to shout something about "hurrying this shit up" when Annie moved.

She changed her grip on Akilah's prosthetic arm and swung it at the man standing next to her.

Hard.

Fletch was on the move before she made contact.

As was Ghost.

And Tex and Fish.

And TJ.

Truck, Wolf, Dude, and the rest of the SEALs pounced as well.

It would've been poetic if it hadn't been so violent.

Not surprisingly, Wolf and his team had the man on their side on the ground and unconscious in seconds.

Fletch and Ghost and their team, had the man in front of *them* down and out before he even knew what was happening as well.

Fish and Tex moved as if they'd been competing in three-legged races their entire lives, reaching the man who'd pushed Annie to the ground at the same time the man across the lawn howled in pain at being hit by Akilah's prosthetic. From what Hollywood said later, Tex punched the man at the same time Fish's foot came out in a classic side kick and took out his knee.

Then TJ was there, ripping the AK-47 out of his lax arms. As soon as the man was on the ground, laying on his back and gasping for air, TJ had the barrel shoved into the man's forehead. "Move one inch, motherfucker, and it'll be the last thing you ever do."

Fletch didn't bother watching whatever TJ was going to do the man, his concern was for his wife and daughter, and the rest of the women.

Obviously he wasn't the only one apprehensive, as Ghost and Coach, along with Tex and Fish, were moving across the lawn.

The last gunman, the one who had been guarding the women, was lying on the ground unconscious, blood pouring from a cut lip, as well as a large gash on his head. One leg was obviously broken, and a bone in his forearm was sticking out of a bloody hole.

Not caring at the moment what happened, how it happened, or who *made* it happen, Fletch went straight for Emily. She was kneeling on the ground holding Annie in her arms, clutching her little head to her chest, making sure she didn't see the violence behind her. Fletch dropped to his knees behind his daughter and engulfed the women who meant more to him than anything else in his life in his embrace.

He felt Emily shudder once, then control it. They stayed like that for several seconds, until Annie wiggled between them and whined, "I can't breathe, Daddy."

Taking a deep breath, more relieved than he could put into words that everyone seemed to be okay, Fletch eased back. He lifted Annie gently from Emily and turned her so she was standing in front of him and they were eye to eye.

"You're okay?" he asked, running his hands up and down her arms.

She nodded.

"You're sure?"

"Yeah, Daddy. I'm sure. Are *you* okay?"

He smiled for the first time since everything had

started. Leave it to Annie to turn the tables and want to make sure *he* was all right.

"I'm okay, sprite."

She turned in his arms then, and called out to Akilah, "Your arm is awesome, Akilah! You're right. It *can* hurt!"

Fletch heard chuckles all around him, but he couldn't take his eyes off his daughter. She was amazing. He put his finger under her chin and brought her face back around to his. "Were you scared?"

She looked into his eyes and said softly, "Not really."

"Why not?"

"Mommy told me once that being scared means you're about to do something really brave. And I want to be brave. Like you."

Fletch's eyes left his daughter's and met Emily's. "Your mommy's pretty smart."

"I know. Just like me," Annie said matter-of-factly.

Not breaking eye contact with his wife, Fletch kissed the top of Annie's head and murmured, "Exactly."

"How 'bout you and me try to sort through everyone's stuff?" a deep voice said to Annie from above their heads.

Fletch looked up to see Dude standing there. He

didn't know the man very well, but there was something in his eyes when he looked at his daughter, that Fletch understood on a basic level. He'd seen it in the church when he'd stood up to move the plastic toys Annie had dropped in the aisle so Emily wouldn't trip over them. Dude was deadly, but he'd never hurt a woman or child. He might be gruff and order them around, but he'd never hurt them.

"Yeah!" Annie answered, and held up her arms toward Dude without hesitation. She'd just met the man today, but apparently she had good intuition when it came to strangers.

Fletch looked up and saw his daughter with both arms around the large SEAL, snuggled into him. He made a mental note to watch her carefully when she started dating. It seemed she had a weakness for alpha men.

"I'll make sure she doesn't see anything," Dude told Fletch gruffly.

"Appreciate it," Fletch said.

Dude nodded, and Fletch saw the man named Mozart come up next to them. The last thing he heard his daughter say was, "You have a scar like Truck does!" and she reached out her tiny hand to pat the other man's cheek.

Fletch would've been exasperated at Annie's penchant to touch and soothe large, scary men who had scars on their faces, but he had more important things to do at the moment.

He turned to Emily and fell back on his butt as she threw herself at him. He gathered her into his arms, managing not to fall to his back. He buried his face into the side of her neck as she did the same to him. They didn't say anything for a long moment, just enjoyed being with each other, safe and unharmed.

When Fletch felt Emily start to shake in his arms, he tightened his hold on her and leaned back so he could see her face. "Em?"

"I'm okay," she reassured him quickly. "It's just adrenaline."

Fletch knew all about that. He ran his hands up and down her back, trying to soothe her.

"Those assholes ruined our wedding," she grumbled quietly.

"No," Fletch said gruffly, "they sure as hell did *not*. Today is our wedding day and I won't let anyone take that from us. This is not the day we almost got robbed. It's *our* day. We will celebrate this day in the future and I'll take you out for dinner then make love to you for hours when we get home. Today is the day I thank God for making you mine."

"That's sweet," Emily murmured.

"No. It's not. It's fact. Everything that happened to those assholes, they asked for. They picked the wrong fucking party to crash and they'll spend a long time in jail regretting it."

"The cameras were on?" Emily asked quietly.

"Of course."

"So the police will see that you guys acted in self-defense?"

Fletch took her head in his hands and forced her to look at him. "What's going on in that head of yours?"

Emily bit her lip then said softly, "I don't want you guys to go to jail."

"We aren't going to jail," Fletch said immediately. "It was clearly self-defense, love. And they're not dead."

"They're not?" Emily asked, one eyebrow raised.

Fletch wanted to be pissed that she thought he'd kill someone in front of Annie, but he understood that she probably wasn't thinking clearly. Besides, he'd told himself not ten minutes earlier that if any of them hurt his girls, he'd kill them without thought. "No. They're just unconscious. I think Penelope was the one who messed up the one guarding you guys the worst."

Emily turned her head to look at the unconscious man nearby. He looked gruesome. Whatever had happened to him had been fast, hard, and brutal. She looked over at Penelope, who was standing next to the firefighter named Moose. He had an arm around her shoulders as they spoke to Beatle and Blade.

"Oh. Has someone called the police?" Emily asked.

"Yeah." Fletch had no idea if that was the truth or not, but figured *someone* had certainly called 911 by now to report what had happened and to let them know an ambulance was needed. If it wasn't one of the civilians, then TJ certainly would've done it. As a law enforcement officer, he'd be on it.

Emily smiled then. A wide, bright smile that lit up his world. "Life is never going to be boring with us, is it?"

Fletch relaxed completely for the first time since the men had shown up with guns. "I highly doubt it."

Chapter Seven

THREE HOURS LATER, the reception had moved indoors. The guests had been interviewed by the police, the bad guys had been arrested and taken away by ambulance to the hospital to be treated. Everyone's belongings had been returned to the rightful owners, including all three of the prosthetics. And most of Fletch and Emily's friends had long since made their way home.

Those left were safely locked inside Fletch's house, lounging or sitting on every available surface. It was a tight fit, but no one seemed to mind.

Tex sat on one end of the couch, Melody tucked into his side, baby Hope sleeping in her arms, and Akilah sitting on the floor in front of them.

Penelope was sitting in one of the large armchairs with Moose sitting on the arm next to her, hovering protectively.

Mary was sitting on the other end of the couch from Tex and Melody, with Truck right next to her. They weren't cuddling, but Mary's usual antagonistic attitude was nowhere to be seen. Instead she looked exhausted.

Ghost and Rayne were sitting on a couple of cushions on the floor, Rayne leaning back into Ghost's chest. Coach and Harley were sitting nearby against a wall, Harley's head on Coach's shoulder, their arms intertwined.

Wolf, Abe, Cookie, TJ, and Fish were sitting at the kitchen table behind the couch, and Mozart, Dude, Benny, Hollywood, Beatle, and Blade were standing in various places around the room.

Annie was sound asleep on the couch next to Truck, her head resting on his massive leg, her knees and arms tucked into her chest.

And lastly, Fletch and Emily sat on the hearth in front of the fireplace. Their clasped hands rested on Fletch's thigh as they decompressed and talked with their friends. It was a large group, and they'd been through a lot over the last eight hours, but no one seemed to be in a hurry to go home, nor had anyone even suggested that the kids be taken off to bed.

"So," Fletch began softly, not wanting to wake up his daughter, "I was a bit busy, someone want to tell me exactly what happened to the asshole guarding the women?" He looked at Penelope as he asked the question.

Her chin went up and she straightened in the

chair. "He underestimated me, that's what happened," she growled.

Fletch chuckled and remarked lightly, "That much is obvious. You fucked him up, Tiger."

She smiled then and relaxed, obviously relieved she wasn't going to have to defend her actions. "Okay, it really wasn't so much me, but I held him still while the others did the dirty work. When Annie hit him with Akilah's arm and distracted him, I went for his gun and we wrestled for it. He was stronger than I was, but my other thought was to keep him from shooting anyone. I didn't have to worry about that for long though, Moose was there almost as soon as I was. He punched the guy in the face while I had my hands on the rifle, splitting his lip, and the guy whipped his rifle up as if to shoot Moose."

Moose took up the story. "I ripped the weapon from his hands and clocked him in the head with it. I went to kick his knee out from under him, but missed and got his thigh instead. I heard the bone snap as my foot connected. He went down."

Then Fish continued the tale. "Tex and I got to him around this time and he'd reached up and was trying to punch Tiger. To prevent her from getting hurt, Tex grabbed his wrist at the same time I kicked at him." The newest member of the group shrugged unapologetically. "It just so happened that his arm was in the way of my foot and it kinda snapped in two and broke through the skin."

"He passed out after that," Tex finished, grinning.

"Thank you for returning my necklace," Penelope told Tex.

Tex nodded at her, giving her a look that said he understood how important it was for her to get the tracker necklace back around her neck as soon as possible.

"Everyone got everything of their own back, right?" Emily asked for the third time.

"Yes, love, everyone got their stuff back," Fletch told her, pulling her to him and kissing the top of her head lovingly.

Emily looked around the room and stated to no one in particular, "I hated giving them my rings. Penelope, I know it hurt for you to take off your necklace. And Tex, Fish, and Akilah, I can't imagine how it felt to have to give up your prosthetics. And I know you guys," she said nodding at each of the Navy SEALs, "didn't expect to have to get into World War III when all you were doing was attending the wedding of a friend. All I can say is that I'm sorry."

"This is not your fault," Fletch growled at the same time almost everyone said the same thing.

Fish stood up from the table and came over to where Emily and Fletch were sitting on the brick hearth. He kneeled down in front of them and said in a low, earnest tone, all the more intense because of the lack of emotion in it, "Your husband and his team saved my life. I wasn't sure I *wanted* my life to be saved at the time, but they did it anyway. Fletch and Truck browbeat me until I finally agreed to come today. I didn't want to. I wanted to lie in my bed at the rehab center and feel sorry for myself. But somehow, after all that happened today, I finally feel like I can crawl out of the dark hole I've been living in for the last few months and reach the top and the sunshine."

"What happened today?" Emily asked softly, not taking her eyes from the tortured soldier in front of her.

"Your daughter happened," Fish said earnestly. "She walked down the aisle happy as a clam in her combat boots dropping flowers and Army men as if it was the most normal thing in the world. And Akilah, a girl who has been though much worse than me, and is a hundred percent happy, made me open my eyes and realize that my life isn't over. And that my dead teammates wouldn't want me to live the rest of my life bitter and pissed off at the world. And your reception got held up by four men who didn't give a shit who they hurt or scared...all in the name of making a few bucks.

"I saw men I respected and trusted in action. I saw

a woman I've never met leap on the back of man with a rifle without a thought to her own safety. I saw a little fucking girl with more bravery in her pinkie finger than most people have in their entire bodies, outsmart a man four times her size. And I saw team-work. Between two groups of soldiers that historically have butted heads when it came to the best way to take down the enemy. It was seamless and selfless and it made me glad to be alive for the first time since I lost my arm."

Emily held her breath as Fish continued.

"So don't be sorry about today, Emily Fletcher. Be thankful for your friends. Be glad that everyone is sitting and standing here safe and sound. Revel in the love of your husband and daughter. Laugh at the fact that the stupid jerks who tried to ruin your day were foiled in grand style and will be behind bars for years to come. Know that you're protected, loved, and that you have good men at your back."

"I know," Emily told Fish in a whisper.

"I'm not better yet. I have a long way to go," Fish said, standing and looking around the room. "But you all have given me hope that I can get there. I'll never be the man or soldier I used to be. But I've realized that it just doesn't matter. *This* is what matters."

Emily heard a few sniffs around her, but didn't take her eyes from Fish. "You're always welcome here,

Dane Munroe. We have a room above our garage. If you need a place to go, you can come here. We won't bother you, you can live there as a hermit for as long as you want."

Fish smiled then. The first real smile Emily had seen on his face. "Thank you, Emily. I appreciate that. But once I'm released from rehab, I'm going west. Maybe Idaho. The fresh air and mountains appeal to me. As does the history of people living there on the fringes of society."

"Just don't become one of those prepper people," Fletch murmured, only half kidding.

Emily jabbed her husband in the side with her elbow, but continued to look at Fish. "I hope you find what you're looking for," Emily told him softly.

"Me too," Fish replied with a heartfelt sigh.

The room was quiet for a long moment, everyone soaking in the conversation between Fish and Emily and simply enjoying being in each other's company. Then Wolf stood up from the table. "On that note, I think we need to get going."

Emily and Fletch stood immediately and Wolf waved them back down.

"Don't get up. We can show ourselves out." He came over to where Emily was still standing and the other SEALs followed him. One by one, as they'd done at the ceremony not so long ago, they leaned down and hugged her goodbye.

Then each went over to Tex and shook his hand, smiling down at his family.

"We should get going too," Moose said quietly to Penelope.

"You're not driving back to San Antonio tonight are you?" Emily asked in concern.

Penelope shook her head. "No. We're staying at a hotel and will head out in the morning." At the wide-eyed surprised look Emily gave her, Penelope quickly clarified, "Not in the same room."

Emily grinned huge at her friend.

"I'm headed back tonight," TJ shared. "I'm used to long shifts in my highway patrol car at night, so the couple of hours it'll take to get home isn't a big deal for me."

"Will you let us know you made it home?" Emily asked.

TJ smiled as if amused by her concern, but merely nodded.

Emily looked over at Rayne and Harley. "I suppose you guys will be leaving too?"

Rayne rolled her eyes. "Yeah, but you know we'll see you in a day or so. It's not like we're going any-where."

"I know, but after what happened tonight, I feel as if you'll be a million miles away."

Rayne's smile died and she walked over to Emily and gave her a huge hug. "Us Delta women have to stick together," she told her in a whisper, still hugging her. "I'll call you tomorrow, okay?"

"Okay," Emily said, relieved.

She gave Harley a hug, then their men too.

The living room almost seemed empty, even though several people were still there.

Mary was still sitting on the couch with Truck at her side and Annie's head in his lap. Tex hadn't moved, so neither had Melody nor their daughters. Hollywood, Beatle, Blade, and Fish were also remained.

"So…who's spending the night?" Emily asked somewhat nervously after the room had cleared out. It was a spontaneous thing to say, especially since it was her wedding night, but for some reason she couldn't bear for *everyone* to disappear. She needed them around. She knew Fletch would keep her safe, but she wanted to have *his* back. And she knew the few men left would, just as they had tonight.

"Tex, you and your family can stay in the garage apartment," Fletch said softly. "Truck and Mary, you're welcome to stay, and you guys," he told his teammates with a head jerk, "can bed down out here."

"I can't spend the night," Mary said immediately, standing up so quickly she swayed on her feet.

"Easy," Truck murmured, catching hold of her elbow, steadying her.

"I'm fine," Mary insisted, jerking her arm out of Truck's grip.

"I'll take you home," Truck told her, easing Annie's head off his lap and standing up next to Mary.

"No. I need my car."

"Why?"

"Because," Mary said stubbornly, glaring at Truck.

"I'll pick you up in the morning and bring you back here to get it," he said evenly.

"That's stupid, Trucker. I'll just drive it home now."

"When's the last time you ate?" he asked weirdly.

Mary's brow scrunched up and she said, "What's that got to do with anything?"

"You're unsteady on your feet. Your skin is pale, and you can barely keep your eyes open. There's no way I'd let you drive home in this condition."

Mary opened her mouth to protest, but Akilah beat her to it. "He is right. You should let him care for you. When you find a good man, you should," she paused as if looking for the right word, then finished, "treasure that."

Mary's mouth closed as if she knew she couldn't argue with the teenager. She looked up at Truck and said quietly, "Okay. I *am* tired, and we need to talk.

Thank you for the ride."

The smile on Truck's face spoke volumes, though no one commented on it. "Thanks. Emily, Fletch, congratulations. I'm so happy you're officially part of our family, even though you were already by default."

"Thanks, Truck," Emily said.

Fletch held out his hand and Truck shook it heartily.

Then there was only Tex, his family, and the Delta guys.

"Go on to bed," Beatle told Fletch and Emily. "You two look exhausted."

"But Annie—" Emily protested.

"I've got her," Beatle said quickly. "I'm getting pretty good at this babysitting thing. It won't be the first time I've put her to bed."

"I put her flower girl basket with her Army men in it by her bed. For whatever reason, they're her favorite toys right now. She pitched a royal little girl fit when we left the church without them."

Beatle grinned. "She wanted to put her own stamp on the wedding," he said, as if he were able to read Annie's mind.

"She sure did." Emily laughed. "If you're sure you're okay with putting her to bed..." Emily said hesitantly.

"I'm sure," Beatle said firmly.

Fletch put his arm around his wife's waist and tugged her into his side. Her arms went around him and she snuggled into his embrace. "Tex, the key to the apartment is on the key rack by the side door. Sheets are clean on the bed, and you can pull out the bed in the sofa. We'll expect you at breakfast in the morning."

The SEAL smiled and nodded. "Wouldn't miss it."

"Thanks for being here," Fletch told him.

Tex got up with the help of his wife and walked to the entryway of the living room with a slight limp. Obviously the day had been harder on him than he was willing to admit. Fletch would've worried about him, but he knew Melody would take good care of her husband. The love between them was easy to see.

Just as they were about to exit the room, Tex turned back and looked at Emily. "Through all that happened today, I didn't get to give you a wedding present."

She opened her mouth to protest, but Tex didn't give her the chance. "Fletch told me that Annie has been begging you guys to let her get her ears pierced. She might be all tomboy now, but I have a feeling by the time she's a teenager, she's gonna be a fashionista. I can't say that I really approve of someone her age getting her ears pierced," he looked down at his infant daughter sleeping peacefully in his wife's arms, then back up at Emily, "but I figured with her big blue doe eyes and cute face, you'll give in sooner rather than later. So I brought her a pair of small pearl studs that she can wear."

"Oh, uh…thanks," Emily stammered, not at all sure how she felt about the present. It wasn't exactly a wedding gift.

Tex smiled as if he knew exactly what she was thinking. "These are a very special pair of earrings, Emily. The kind that will help you, and someone you know and hopefully trust, to keep tabs on your daughter at all times. We live in a sick, crazy world, and I know for a fact when Hope gets old enough to be mobile, she'll have her own pair."

Akilah spoke up then. "And I have some too," she said, brushing her hair back and showing off the small blue stones in her ears.

Tex smiled at his daughter and put his hand on her head lovingly. Then he said softly, "Goodnight, everyone. We'll see you in the morning. Congratulations again, you two." And with that, Tex and his family left the room.

Emily immediately turned to Fletch. "What was that about?"

He smiled down at her and didn't beat around the bush. "The earrings have tracking devices in them, love."

"What?"

"The same kind of tracker that's in Tiger's necklace that she never takes off. The same thing all the SEAL wives wear every day. Tex giving that to Annie is his way of letting us know that we'll never have to worry about her disappearing. Ever."

"I'm not sure I'm comfortable with that. I feel like it's spying on her." Emily chewed on her lip in indecision.

"We won't have access to the data, love. Just Tex will. Remember how you felt when Jacks kidnapped you? Well, if anyone ever dares to try anything like that with our daughter, we can be there before anything bad happens."

"Well, jeez, when you put it that way," Emily mumbled.

Fletch chuckled. "You don't have to decide right away. Think about it."

"I will."

Fletch nodded and kissed the top of her head. "Make yourselves at home, guys," Fletch told Hollywood, Beatle, and Blade, who were unabashedly eavesdropping on their conversation and grinning. "Don't bother me unless the house is burning down," he added.

"Wouldn't dream of it, man," Blade said with a

smirk.

"Before you go off and enjoy yourselves, Mr. and Mrs. Fletcher, can I have your Wi-Fi code? I want to check my email." Hollywood said.

"Really? Anyone we know?" Fletch asked, before giving his friend their Internet code.

Hollywood smiled and shook his head. "No, but hopefully you'll meet her at the Army Ball in a few weeks. We've been messaging back and forth for a while now...and I like her. She's honest and refreshing to talk to."

"Cool," Emily told him with a grin. "What's her name?"

"Kassie," Hollywood told her, but didn't elaborate.

"I can't wait to meet her. You sound...serious about this one."

Hollywood shrugged, but his lips twitched up into a small smile. "I think I am."

"Awesome," Emily told him earnestly. Then she looked at the others. "Anyone else need anything?"

"We'll be fine. Go," Beatle ordered, sitting on the couch next to the still-sleeping Annie. "We'll just hang out for a while and watch television...you know...so we won't be able to hear anything."

Emily blushed and wrapped her arm around her husband's waist.

Narrowing his eyes at Beatle, admonishing him

without words for embarrassing Emily, Fletch merely nodded and steered her down the hall to their room.

He might've been embarrassed to be spending his wedding night with his friends down the hall, but with all the team had been through together, them knowing he was balls deep inside his wife was low on his give-a-shit meter.

Fletch could feel Emily's curves against him as they headed down the hallway to the master bedroom. He'd licked, kissed, and caressed every one of those curves, but the thought of making love to her—in bed, lying down and taking his time—sent his heart racing into overdrive. The quickie earlier had taken the edge off and been nice, but now it was time to show Emily how much he loved her and that she'd made him the happiest man alive today.

Chapter Eight

FOR SOME REASON, Emily was nervous. She stood in their bathroom and ran her hands down the front of the ivory nightie she was wearing. Rayne had given it to her as a wedding present and it was beautiful. It had spaghetti straps and a deep vee in front, showing off the inside curves of both breasts. It clung to her waist and hips and flared out just a bit over her ass. It was short. Really short. Coming to mid-thigh. The back was completely bare down to her ass crack, and was only held together by a tie at the middle of her spine.

Surprisingly, or not, it wasn't that comfortable. The lace at the edge of the bodice was scratchy and she felt extremely exposed...which she supposed was the point. Emily knew without a doubt she wouldn't be wearing the slinky material for long, but still.

She knew Fletch thought she'd be coming to bed wearing the undergarments she'd had on under her wedding dress, but she liked the thought of surprising him.

It was silly to be nervous about walking into the room she shared with Fletch. He'd seen her naked, of course he had, but it seemed different tonight. Maybe it was because of what had happened earlier and knowing that the night could've ended up very different if anyone had been seriously hurt. Maybe it was the weight of her wedding ring back on her finger, where it felt like it belonged. Taking a deep breath, Emily let it out slowly. She took one last look at herself in the mirror and nodded. She wanted her husband. It was time.

She pushed open the bathroom door and walked into the bedroom—and stopped in her tracks and gazed around in disbelief. While she'd been getting ready, Fletch had been busy.

There were small votive candles everywhere, flickering in the slight breeze from the ceiling fan. The comforter had been pulled back invitingly on their bed and rose petals were on the sheets. Not a lot, but enough to let her know that her new husband had gone to quite a bit of trouble to try to make the night perfect.

And speaking of her new husband, Fletch was standing next to the bed in nothing but a pair of boxer briefs. She hungrily took him in from head to toe. His hair was adorably mussed, his broad shoulders and biceps rippled as he stood and stared back at her. The tattoos on his arms seemed even sexier in the low light…and maybe because it was their wedding night. His trim waist led to his groin, where it was more than obvious he was eager for their night to start. His thick thigh muscles flexed as he took a step toward her, then another, until he was right in front of her.

"Jesus, Em, you're always beautiful, but tonight you take my breath away. I thought your corset was sexy, but this…damn. Turn," he ordered, lifting a hand and swirling his index finger in a circle.

Emily turned, intending it to be a quick spin because she hadn't had enough of looking at her husband, but he stopped her with the simple action of putting his hands on her waist and holding her still when her back was to him.

"Fuck. Me," he breathed, and Emily felt his warm breath on the back of her neck. Goosebumps rippled down her body and she closed her eyes.

Fletch used a finger to trace the straps of the nightie from one side to the other, then returned to the bow and leaned over, kissing his way up the middle of her spine to her neck. Emily's head dropped, giving him access to her nape.

"This is the sexiest thing I've ever seen," Fletch uttered, more to himself than her. His finger traced her spine again, going over the bow in the middle and continuing down until it nestled in the crack of her ass.

Emily shifted in his grasp, pushing her butt back against him. His hand moved to her belly and pulled her flush against him. He was hot. Radiating heat.

Emily brought one hand up and laid it over his on her stomach, and reached back with the other to tangle her fingers in his hair. "I love you, Cormac."

"I love you too, Miracle Emily. You're *my* miracle. You and Annie. You have no idea."

"Oh, I think I have some idea," Emily murmured, fidgeting in front of him, getting more turned on by the second.

She spun in his arms, knowing the only reason she was able to was because he let her. Fletch wasn't necessarily dominant in bed, but he did tend to be a bit bossy. He had a tendency to move her where he wanted, when he wanted, and most of the time it didn't matter if *she* wanted something, he'd make her wait until *he* was ready to give it to her.

But she could tell that tonight he was on the edge. Just as she was. The adrenaline that had flowed through her veins, making her jittery and even a bit desperate to feel her husband inside her, had to be coursing through his body too.

Emily lifted her arms until her hands were clasped behind his neck and said softly, "The room is perfect, thank you."

"Since we weren't going to a hotel or anything, I wanted to make it special for you," Fletch said quietly, his hands in constant motion, rubbing up and down her back, along her sides, brushing against the sides of her breasts, and even dipping down under her nightie to cup her ass and press her hips into his own.

"Every minute of every day I get to spend with you is special," she told him. "But right now the only thing I can think about is making love with my husband."

Without a word, he took a step backwards, holding her to him so she had no choice but to step forward. He did it again, then again, until they were standing next to their bed. Still not speaking with his lips, but saying volumes with his eyes, Fletch sat on the edge of the mattress, and reached around her, grabbing hold of one of the strings to the tie at her back and pulling slowly and steadily.

Emily felt the material sag when the bow was undone and smiled when Fletch's eyes dilated with lust. She shrugged one shoulder, letting the strap fall, then did the same with the other. The ivory material fell to her feet with a soft whoosh and she was standing naked in front of her husband.

Fletch spread his legs and pulled Emily forward until she was right in front of him. He put one hand on the small of her back, his little finger nestling once more in the crack of her ass, and placed the other at the side of her neck, his thumb caressing her jaw.

Looking up, he said softly, "I love you, Em. So much it scares me sometimes. Simply knowing you're waiting for me when I get off work makes me feel a contentment I never thought I'd have. When I wake up in the mornings, the first thing I do is look for you sleeping next to me. I've spent many a night, and morning, watching you sleep, and knowing I'm the luckiest bastard to ever walk this earth. Thank you for trusting me. Even when you thought I was working with that asshole, Jacks, a part of you knew I wouldn't hurt you. And I won't. Ever. I was so scared tonight. Not for me, but for you. And our daughter. I can't live without you, Em. I swear to God, I can't."

"And you don't have to. I feel the same way about you, Fletch. Women like me don't get men like you. No, don't get offended," she soothed when he frowned up at her. "I'm just saying you could have any woman in the world, but you chose me. I don't, and will never, take that for granted."

Fletch moved then, grabbing his wife by the waist and standing and twisting at the same time until she was lying on her back on the bed, and he was hovering over her. Emily could feel his hard length against her slick pussy and she wanted him inside her more than she wanted to breathe. She shifted and tilted her hips upward, pressing herself against him.

"I want you inside me," she said softly, putting her hands under his waistband and pushing down as far as she could reach, which wasn't far. "Take these off," she ordered.

Fletch smiled and complied. Shifting to the side and stripping his underwear off in a move that would've been impressive if she'd been paying attention. But all Emily could see was her husband, hard and as desperate for her as she was for him.

He came back over her, and Emily widened her legs, letting him settle between them. One of his hands eased down her body to her center, testing her readiness. He grinned down at her when he found her already slick with want.

Without a word, he grabbed the base of his cock and fitted it to her opening. Emily lifted her knees and put her feet on the backs of his thighs, fully opening herself to him.

Slowly, too slowly, Fletch pressed his length inside her. He was gentle, letting her get used to him, but he didn't stop until his balls were pressed against her body.

Emily wiggled and lifted her hips, taking him deeper.

They both sighed in ecstasy.

Still without words, Fletch eased out of her, then pushed back in. He did it again, then again.

"Faster," Emily begged, pressing her heels into the backs of his thighs.

"No," he said, shaking his head to emphasize his point. "I fucked my wife earlier, now I want to make love to her."

"You *are*," Emily whined. "But I want you to go faster."

"And *I* want it to last," Fletch countered, continuing his slow, easy pace.

"We have the rest of our lives, Fletch," Emily told him. "You can make love to me later."

He grinned, but didn't speed up his thrusts. "But every time I try to make love to you, you get impatient and want me to go faster."

Damn him, he was right. Emily tightened her internal muscles when he pushed inside her the next time and was pleased with the small groan that escaped his mouth.

"You don't play fair," he grumbled, mock glaring at her.

"As good as this feels, you know how I like it best," she informed him, because he did. She could usually only get off when he was pounding into her. She needed direct stimulation on her clit, and she loved it the most when he took her hard at the same time he manipulated her directly.

He sighed as if he was deeply perturbed, but Emily

knew it was an act. He loved when he could let himself go and pound into her almost as much as she did.

Fletch rolled, taking her with him, until she was perched on top of him. "Fine, wife, take me as you want."

Emily grinned. She might be on top, but he was still fully in control and they both knew it. She immediately began to lift up and and down on his hard cock, jerking when she felt his thumb press on her clit. She ground herself down on him, pushing forward, trying to get him to press harder on her bundle of nerves.

"Fuck me, wife," Fletch ordered softly, lifting his other hand to engulf her breast and pinch her nipple.

So she did. Hard and fast. Just like she wanted to in the first place. Grinding down on her husband as if she was starring in a porn film. She hunched forward, bracing herself with her hands on his stomach, and fucked him for all she was worth. Within minutes, she was coming. Jerking and quaking over him, moaning and curling her fingernails into his chest as she went over the top.

And when he continued to rub her clit, not stopping as he usually did when she came, Emily exploded again...or kept on coming, she wasn't sure which. God, it felt so good and hurt all at the same time. "Fletch," she gasped.

"Fuck, you're beautiful," she heard him say before he palmed her ass with the hand that had been at her breast and pulled her down into him at the same time his hips thrust up.

The groans that came out of his mouth were also porn star worthy, and Emily felt another mini orgasm ripple through her pussy as he filled her with his come.

She could feel his cock flexing inside her as he came down from his orgasm and she slowly lowered her body until she was draped over him.

The scent of roses and sex filled her nostrils. The flower petals now crushed under them, but Emily didn't care. She buried her nose in the crook of Fletch's neck and sighed, loving the goosebumps that formed on his arms as she did. Rubbing her palms up and down his biceps, Emily said softly, "I love you."

"Not as much as I love you," Fletch returned immediately in a husky whispered tone.

They said nothing more, simply enjoying being in each other's arms, letting their heartbeats return to normal. Emily dozed, only stirring lightly when Fletch turned them, his expended cock slipping out of her body as he did.

She grumbled, but settled when he curled himself around her and pulled the sheet up to cocoon them in the warm cavern that was their bed.

"Annie," Emily murmured, knowing their daughter had a habit of waking them in the mornings by bursting into their room and joining them in bed for early morning snuggles.

"Shhhh. I'll wake you up later so you can put something on," Fletch reassured her.

"Kay."

"Happy zero anniversary, love," Fletch said, and kissed her temple.

"I like that," Emily whispered.

"Good. Now sleep."

Emily was out before the last word left his mouth.

FLETCH WATCHED HIS wife sleep, just as he did most nights. Even after all the time they'd been together, it was still tough to believe she was his.

Their relationship wasn't perfect, it was hectic and they occasionally sniped at each other. Emily didn't like to spend money they didn't have to, as a result of the way she'd spent the last seven years living from paycheck to paycheck, and they'd sometimes fight about him buying both her and Annie things, but Fletch wouldn't change one thing about their relationship.

Emily was generally a positive person. She didn't dwell on things that she couldn't control...like his work schedule. If he called at the last minute and said he wouldn't be home until late, or that he would be leaving for a mission and didn't know when he'd be home, it didn't seem to bother her. He knew she worried about him, but she never told him she hated his job or tried to get him to quit. If Annie got sick, they discussed together who would stay home with her. When he needed space because of a rough mission or needed to plan *for* a mission, she seemed to understand and kept Annie out of his way until he'd worked through whatever he needed to. Then they'd talk about what was bothering them late at night when they were in bed. Neither of them was perfect, but they were making it work.

Fletch brushed a lock of Emily's hair behind her ear and smiled, thinking about their wedding. Annie had been adorable. Emily radiant. And they'd gotten to spend the day with their friends and family.

Besides the stupid assholes who thought robbing wedding receptions would be a way to make easy money, the day had been perfect. He kissed Emily's temple once more then snuggled in next to his wife. *His wife.* God he loved that.

His teammates had questioned him adopting Annie before he and Emily were married, but he and Emily had talked about it before they'd followed through. She'd told him that she trusted him enough to allow him to officially make her little girl his before they tied the knot.

"She loves you, and even if something happens between us, and we don't end up getting married, I can't imagine you ever letting her down."

Fletch had reassured her that nothing would ever happen to break them up, and yes, he'd always take care of and protect Annie. It was unorthodox, but she'd given him the go-ahead to adopt her daughter and officially make her his.

Fletch didn't know what the future held. Not for him and Emily. Not for his daughter. Not for his teammates and friends. Watching the various relationship dynamics play out that day had been amusing, but one thing he knew for sure.

No one would ever be happier than he was right this moment.

The last thought Fletch had before he fell into a contented sleep was that he couldn't wait for tomorrow to start...simply because the two females he loved more than life itself would be there at his side, experiencing it with him.

Look for the next book in the *Delta Force Heroes* Series, *Rescuing Kassie*.

<u>To sign up for Susan's Newsletter go to:</u>
http://bit.ly/SusanStokerNewsletter

<u>Or text:</u> STOKER to 24587 for text alerts on your
mobile device

Discover other titles by Susan Stoker

Delta Force Heroes

Rescuing Rayne

Assisting Aimee – Loosely related to Delta Force

Rescuing Emily

Rescuing Harley

Marrying Emily

Rescuing Kassie (May 2017)

Rescuing Bryn (Nov 2017)

Rescuing Casey (TBA)

Rescuing Wendy (TBA)

Rescuing Mary (TBA)

Badge of Honor: Texas Heroes

Justice for Mackenzie

Justice for Mickie

Justice for Corrie

Justice for Laine

Shelter for Elizabeth

Justice for Boone

Shelter for Adeline

Shelter for Sophie (Aug 2017)

Justice for Erin (Nov 2017)

Justice for Milena (TBA)

Shelter for Blythe (TBA)

Justice for Hope (TBA)

Shelter for Quinn (TBA)

Shelter for Koren (TBA)
Shelter for Penelope (TBA)

SEAL of Protection

Protecting Caroline
Protecting Alabama
Protecting Fiona
Marrying Caroline
Protecting Summer
Protecting Cheyenne
Protecting Jessyka
Protecting Julie
Protecting Melody
Protecting the Future
Protecting Alabama's Kids
Protecting Kiera (June 2017)
Protecting Dakota (Sept 2017)

Ace Security

Claiming Grace (Mar 2017)
Claiming Alexis (July 2017)
Claiming Bailey (TBA)

Beyond Reality

Outback Hearts
Flaming Hearts
Frozen Hearts

Connect with Susan Online

__Susan's Facebook Profile and Page:__
www.facebook.com/authorsstoker
www.facebook.com/authorsusanstoker

__Follow Susan on Twitter:__
www.twitter.com/Susan_Stoker

__Find Susan's Books on Goodreads:__
www.goodreads.com/SusanStoker

__Email:__ Susan@StokerAces.com

__Website:__ www.StokerAces.com

__To sign up for Susan's Newsletter go to:__
http://bit.ly/SusanStokerNewsletter

__Or text:__ STOKER to 24587 for text alerts on your
mobile device

.

About the Author

New York Times, *USA Today*, and *Wall Street Journal* Bestselling Author Susan Stoker has a heart as big as the state of Texas, where she lives, but this all-American girl has also spent the last fourteen years living in Missouri, California, Colorado, and Indiana. She's married to a retired Army man who now gets to follow *her* around the country.

She debuted her first series in 2014 and quickly followed that up with the SEAL of Protection Series, which solidified her love of writing and creating stories readers can get lost in.

If you enjoyed this book, or any book, please consider leaving a review. It's appreciated by authors more than you'll know.

CPSIA information can be obtained
at www.ICGtesting.com
Printed in the USA
BVOW06s0942190117
473934BV00002B/2/P